I0453050

CARTER'S HEART CONDITION

JANICE L. DENNIE

KENTE ROMANCE
An Imprint of Kente Publications
P.O. Box 184
Jackson, CA 95642

Copyright © 2015 Janice L. Dennie
ISBN-10: 0964334991
ISBN-13: 9780964334991

All rights reserved. No portion of this book may be reproduced or transmitted in any form or by any electronic or mechanical means, including photocopying, recording or by any informational retrieval and storage systems without permission of the publisher.

Names, characters and incidents depicted in this book are products of the author's imagination, or are used in a fictitious situation. Any resemblances to actual events, locations, organizations, incidents or persons–living or dead–are coincidental and beyond the intent of the author.

THE UNDERWOOD FAMILY

Frank Underwood & Henrietta Underwood
Children:
-Joseph Underwood

Joseph Underwood & Jewell Underwood
Children:
-Kenton Underwood
-Justin Underwood
-Carter Underwood
-Brandon Underwood
-Crystal Underwood

Joshua Underwood & Eunice Underwood
Children:
-Daniel Underwood
-Delores Underwood

Frank and Joshua are brothers.

Daniel Underwood & Angela Underwood
Children:
-Tisha Underwood
-Jason Underwood

You can enjoy CARTER'S HEART CONDITION as a standalone or read it as part of the series.

Dear Reader:

I enjoyed writing Carter & Courtney's story. Hard-driving, self-centered CEO, Carter Underwood like so many of us believes he must search the world over to find happiness and never looks in his own backyard.

Courtney, like so many women, is a resilient character who bounces back from all of the hard knocks life throws her way. But she doesn't wallow in her misfortune. She does what many do in such situations. She gets back up, dusts herself off and keeps on steppin'. When you pair a resilient woman like Courtney with a hard driving, self-centered CEO like Carter, what happens? Fireworks as spectacular as the Fourth of July!

Sit back, relax and enjoy reading Carter & Courtney's book.

Janice

Chapter 1

"I'm taking a leave of absence," he stated firmly in the private meeting.

Carter Underwood, CEO of Underwood Technologies, sat around a coffee table in his two thousand square foot Silicon Valley office, with a look of an Ironman laboratory, a garage, and a living room. He stared at his inner-circle of executives—Reginald Ainsworth, Chairman of the Board and Dr. Sandeep Gupta, Medical Advisor, from under straight dark brows set below short black hair fading into long thin sideburns.

"Carter, I'm merely saying, you should re-think taking a leave of absence right now. We have a good thing going here. You should spend more time inventing new devices instead of taking time off running around the world." Reginald said before standing up to leave.

"You know me, Reginald. When I make up my mind to do something, there's no turning back."

"Have you completed the software to run your artificial liver?" Reginald asked, his eyes narrowing.

"I finished the software yesterday. All I need to do is test it."

"But what about the rest of your inventions you have coming down the line?"

Carter sighed. "You don't get it, Reggie? I'm done with spending my entire life in this workshop developing more medical devices to earn more money."

"What's wrong with earning money? You thought it was a good idea when we were in college," Reginald countered.

"First of all, Reginald, I don't have a problem with earning money. I have a problem working twenty-four hours a day like a machine! Right now, I have more money than I can count. But with you Reginald—enough is never enough. I never realized how greedy you are until now. Give me a break man."

"Guys, guys. Let's take a break while we're ahead." Sandeep interrupted the heated exchange of words between his two college roommates. "The last thing I want to see is you two getting into a fist fight like you used to in college."

"Why do you want to leave Carter? Talk to me," Sandeep pleaded.

Carter glared at his best friend. "I want to take some time off to travel and get a new perspective on my life."

Six months earlier, Carter's mother died leaving

him devastated. He'd been unable to sleep or relax for months. He'd spent his every waking hour working in his lab until he decided to change his empty, self-centered, lifestyle, believing there had to be a better way of living.

Sandeep smiled at Carter giving him a sympathetic look. "I support whatever makes you happy."

Carter knew Sandeep wouldn't have a problem with his decision. But Reginald, on the other hand, reacted the way Carter expected. Reginald enjoyed making money off of Carter's lucrative inventions.

"Have you thought about who's going to take your place while you are away?" Reginald asked sarcastically.

"I want Sandeep to handle my duties while I'm away. Would you mind, Deep?"

"I'd be honored," Sandeep said.

Reginald looked at his watch and saw it was nine o'clock. "Today is Friday. I need to get back to my office. I have a lunch meeting with an advertising firm."

Sandeep stood up to leave. "Don't worry about the corporation. I've got your back. I'll see you at the wedding tomorrow."

"I'm taking the helicopter from my house. Want

a ride."

"No. But thanks. I have to pick up my daughter from soccer practice."

Carter touched Sandeep's shoulder. "Deep, make sure you hire more bioengineers from Stanford. They are trained to do what I do."

"I will Carter, but I'll never find anyone as gifted as you," Sandeep said. "Nonetheless, my friend, your happiness comes first in my book. I'll get Human Resources to recruit some more bioengineers from Stanford next week."

"Thanks, Deep. I knew I could count on you." Carter walked over to his desk after they left and gazed at the clear blue sky through his floor to ceiling windows. He plopped into his executive chair and swiveled around to face his laptop.

An hour later, with a pencil clenched between his teeth, Carter entered the last line of code to operate his artificial liver. He pressed the enter key to test his software, and then his cell phone rang. As a tech genius, Carter hated distractions when he was wired into the zone because it always took him another thirty minutes to get back in.

After his cell phone had ringed several more times, Carter tore his eyes away from his laptop screen to see who was calling. It was his grandmother. He sighed. If he didn't pick up the phone, she'd keep calling.

He took a deep breath. Granny, I love you, but I'm busy right now. He knew she wanted to talk about his brother's wedding this weekend. I'll call you back later, he promised silently.

After he had finished testing his software, he leaned back in his chair, clasped his hands behind his head and exhaled. "Whew! I'm finally finished," he huffed. He waited for any error messages. His program came back with two error messages. He cursed under his breath.

Grabbing his cell phone, he walked to the coffee machine and brewed himself a cup of coffee.

Carter's time was precious. He didn't want to spend all day in traffic—he wanted to spend the day with his brothers at his family's winery in Napa. Picking up his cell phone, he texted Tre, his account manager at Air Charter Service and scheduled a helicopter flight from his home to the Napa Airport. He gave Tre all of the details for the trip.

After drinking his coffee, he packed up his laptop and drove his Tesla sedan to his home in Hillsborough. Once he arrived home, he pulled out his tuxedo and laid it across his bed. While packing his overnight bag, he heard his cell phone ring. He picked up the phone and saw his grandmother's name again.

"Hello Granny."

"Hello to you too, Grandson," Henrietta

Underwood said with her raspy voice. "I'm calling to find out what time you're coming?"

Carter pulled out a pair of dress shoes, underwear, a few polo shirts and khaki trousers while he talked to his grandmother. "I meant to return your call earlier, but I was in the middle of testing some new software. I'm packing right now, Granny."

"Are you bringing a date?"

A date? Carter lowered his head for a second thinking about the women he'd paid to attend business functions with him to keep his personal life uncomplicated. "No, Granny. I'm not bringing a date. But I'll be spending the night in my old room at the house. I'll see you later this afternoon."

Though Carter possessed the Underwood good looks, he'd come to believe women wanted him for two reasons—his money or his time. Time meant money to Carter, and he hated distractions that took him away from his work. He never spent much time pursuing women. In fact, women pursued him, especially after they found out who he was and his financial standing.

"Good. I'll look for you at around four o'clock," Henrietta said.

"Okay. See you then, Granny."

Courtney Oliver packed the last of her clothing

into a large storage box. She left two dresses hanging in her bedroom closet—a sleeveless navy dress and a soft mint spandex dress she would wear to her friend's wedding tomorrow. She'd spent all morning packing boxes and cleaning her three-bedroom home in the exclusive Oakland Hills.

Before the Great Recession, Courtney owned two pieces of property. Her home in the hills and a duplex apartment building in the flatlands she'd paid off shortly after graduating from college.

It had been six months since she'd been laid off as a fourth-grade teacher at Martin Luther King Elementary School. The school district said she'd be called back within a few months. Still waiting to hear from the school, Courtney decided to fall back on her skills as a freelance graphic artist to supplement her income.

Six years ago Courtney had adopted her newborn nephew Gabriel, who was spending the weekend with her sick mother. Courtney had adopted him to prevent him being placed into foster care by Family Protective Services when her sister abandoned him for drugs.

After Courtney's lifestyle had changed, she noticed one of her few friends who kept in touch was Ashley Jacobs, her sorority sister who was getting married tomorrow. Nothing could keep Courtney away from Ashley's wedding.

Courtney's ponytail bounced against the back of

her yoga outfit as she walked outside and posted a For Sale sign in her front yard hoping for a quick sell before the bank foreclosed on her home with a million dollar view of the San Francisco Bay.

Courtney showered and put on her navy blue dress and matching fabric stilettos. She couldn't imagine going to Napa Valley without tasting wine from new and exciting wineries offering free tastings. She'd made arrangements to stay at a bed and breakfast, before being laid off. She tried to cancel her reservation, but the steep cancelation fee was more expensive than staying one night, so she decided to make the best of it, and charged the room to her credit card. Spending a weekend in Napa would allow her to attend Ashley's wedding on Saturday and spend Sunday tasting wine before returning to Oakland.

After ensuring the house was in pristine condition, Courtney stood at the front door one last time, looked around and softly closed the door to a lifestyle that had fallen off a cliff.

***

It was six o'clock in the early evening when Courtney drove past a neighborhood of elegantly restored homes in downtown Napa's Historic District. She drove up the driveway to the Sutton House, a quaint bed, and breakfast located in downtown Napa within walking distance to restaurants, wineries and art galleries.

Courtney parked her Lexus sedan in the parking lot and took a look around. She inhaled the fresh, clean air and exhaled, admiring the casual stone structure. A weekend in Napa was what she needed to relax and get away from the stress of her situation. She walked to the back of her car, popped her trunk and pulled out her bags. After walking up the stone steps, she opened the front door into a craftsman style foyer. She looked to her left and saw the living room painted in a rich hunter green accented with a large stone fireplace flanked by two Queen Anne chairs upholstered in a green and tan tapestry. She could see the dining room through wide opening. She walked up to the reception desk and saw an attractive middle-aged woman wearing a multicolored silk cardigan, and black wide leg pants.

"May I help you?" The woman asked.

Courtney smiled at the woman with short, silver curly hair. "I have a room reservation. My name is Courtney Oliver."

"Yes, I see your name right here," the woman said, admiring Courtney's simple sleeveless navy dress. She checked her name on the computer screen. "You have a king size room reserved."

Courtney looked at her name badge and politely corrected her. "No, Victoria. I reserved a room with two queen beds."

"I'm sorry, for the mix up, Dear, but the last

room we have left is a king room."

Courtney exhaled. "Okay. I'll take it." She had planned to share the room with her sorority sister to cut down on expenses.

Biting her bottom lip, Victoria said, "I feel obligated to make up for the mistake. I'll personally make sure your stay here is comfortable. You can leave your bags here. I'll have someone bring them up to your room shortly. Please, follow me."

Courtney followed Victoria up the staircase to a room on the second floor. She opened the door to a spotlessly clean room with stylish white bedding covering a large fluffy featherbed. She looked around and saw elegant linens in the bath and plenty of privacy.

"We have a spa room downstairs where we offer massages." Victoria stated, watching Courtney inspect the room while checking messages on her cell phone. "We offer gourmet breakfast any time of the day, and complimentary wine and cheese in the dining room every evening. I can have someone turn down your bed at night and bring in a complimentary bottle of champagne, chocolate-covered strawberries, candles, and music."

Courtney looked up from her cell phone. "Thank you, Victoria, but those items won't be necessary. I'm spending the weekend alone to attend a wedding tomorrow."

"You wouldn't be going to the Underwood-Jacobs wedding would you?"

"Yes. You know them?"

"Very well. I'll be attending the wedding also."

Courtney smiled, "Thank you, Victoria, for your help."

"You're welcome. Call the front desk if you need anything." Victoria turned around and left.

Courtney sat on the edge of the bed and texted Melanie apologizing about the mix up with the accommodations. Melanie texted her back saying she didn't mind not spending the night. They made arrangements to sit together at the wedding and socialize at the reception. They continued texting back and forth.

"I guess our Sunday wine tasting date is canceled," Courtney texted.

"Yes. Looks like we need to cancel, but we can always come back another time."

Courtney ended the text and picked up the tour book to find out where she was going to have dinner when she heard a knock on her door. The bell boy with her bags walked in. He hung up her mint green dress and rolled her bag by the closet.

Carter looked out the helicopter window at the big H inside the helipad circle at the private corporate Airport in Napa. He saw his limousine parked in front of a group of hangars in the distance. After exiting the helicopter, Carter turned around and waved goodbye to the pilot he knew on a first name basis. The limousine driver pulled up to Carter, took his bags and put them in the trunk. Carter arrived at his family's five thousand acre winery at dusk. He buttoned up his linen blazer to ward off the spring chill about to set in since the sun was setting. He walked into the winery, passing the gift store, offices, delicatessen, and the hospitality center where event planners were still decorating in preparation for the wedding reception.

He knew where his brothers would be, right where he found them—in the lounge relaxing next to the fireplace.

Kenton and Justin were sitting in a group of six chairs surrounding a round cocktail table. They stood up to greet their brother.

"What's up, Bros?" Carter said as he walked into the lounge wearing a pair of khaki slacks and a purple polo shirt. He tossed his navy linen blazer on an empty chair.

"Carter! How have you been?" Kenton said as he hugged Carter.

"I'm fine Bro."

"You know I need my hug," Justin said, holding out his arms, his smile revealing a deep dimple in his left cheek.

"Hey, Justin. You getting excited?"

"Excited is not the word," Justin said as they all sat down taking a seat around the table.

"Where's Ashley?" Carter asked.

"She's at the spa with her sister and the flower girl getting all glammed up for the wedding."

"She doesn't need to get glammed up. She's already gorgeous."

"Thanks, man," Justin grinned. "If you ever get a chance, Carter, you should get her Aloha Massage."

"A massage sounds relaxing. I can't wait. Where's Briana and my nephew, Jonathan?" Carter asked Kenton.

Kenton took a sip of his drink. "She's at Poppy Hill preparing a fabulous dinner for the family and the bridal party tonight. Jonathan is with her. He's fine."

Carter's jaw twitched. He'd always felt ignored by his older brothers, but never complained. Since they were both blessed with intelligent, accomplished brides, Carter felt like they were leaving him in the dust. His thoughts led to old wounds opening up.

Growing up in a house full of brothers, Carter felt crowded out. He felt like there was no place for him to fit in the family—nothing he could do was wanted or needed. Kenton was the protective one, Justin was the strong one and Brandon, was the artistic one. Everyone had something to contribute to the family except him. As a result, Carter sought out something he could bring to the table. He looked in areas his brothers had not already explored and found he was gifted in science and technology. After he had found his calling, his grandmother dubbed him the gifted one because of his gift of genius.

Justin scrubbed a hand over his face reading Carter's mind. "I know you've felt left out of the family for years Carter." Justin said remembering how he and Kenton used to ignore Carter when he was a boy.

Kenton gave Carter a sad look. "We were wrong, Brother."

"I'm sorry, Carter. I should have included you in the wedding from the beginning," Justin said.

"I should have included you in mine too," Kenton said.

"I'm okay, Brothers. Let's not get depressed. Today is supposed to be a happy day. Both of you have gorgeous wives. I wish I could find a woman like Briana or Ashley," Carter said.

"Sounds like an excuse, Carter?" Kenton said.

"An excuse?" Carter looked up. "What do you mean?"

"I've never seen you with a woman, Carter. Admit it, you're not attracted to women."

"Are you crazy? I am too attracted to women." He paused for a second. "I haven't met one I can trust."

"I used to have trust issues until I met Briana." Kenton said.

"Yeah, but, the women I seem to meet are groupies and gold diggers." More than anything, Carter wanted to meet an honest woman.

"All women are not distrustful. Sometimes you have to step out on faith."

Carter raised his eyebrows. "I have faith. But I rely on logic."

Kenton rolled his eyes at Carter's egghead mentality. He'd never seen Carter with a woman. "Let me ask you a question, Carter. Have you ever been in love?" Kenton asked.

"Love. No." Carter's stomach rolled when he said the word, love. He believed a loving relationship was not in the cards for him.

"I know what's wrong with you," Kenton said. "You're suffering from a heart condition."

"A heart condition? What's that?"

"It's when your heart is in scrap condition. You may need to get it refitted."

"And just how do I get my heart refitted? Take it to a body shop?" Carter asked sarcastically.

"No. Your heart is like an engine, Brother. If you don't rev it up every now and then, it will conk out on you. All it will be good for is scrap. Haven't you seen those lonely people who've lived wasted lives? You have to open up your heart and use it, Brother," Kenton advised.

Carter laughed. "Well, that's a new one on me." He laughed the joke off, but he knew Kenton was right. He couldn't recall ever being in love.

"Tell me, Kenton, how does it feel to be in love?"

"To be in love feels like being in heaven. Your life can become a heaven or hell depending on the partner you choose. I love everything about Briana—her Low Country cooking, her sweet southern accent, and her hard-headed independent spirit. I love the way she challenges me when I'm wrong. She is my best friend, a person who I can tell things I've never told anyone else. I need her in my life as much as I need air to breathe. That's how love makes me feel, Carter."

"What about you Justin, what does it feel like to be in love with Ashley?"

"I fell in love with Ashley when I first heard her sweet voice. She had the voice of an angel. When she was stuck in the earthquake last year, I got down on my knees and prayed she wasn't dead. When you meet your special woman, you'll know the moment you see her."

Kenton looked up and saw Brandon and Crystal walk in. "Come on everybody. Everyone is here, let's go have dinner at Poppy Hill."

Chapter 2

Carter and Sandeep sat at the bar in the crowded hospitality room inside the winery. They were trying to hold a conversation over three hundred elegantly dressed guests, eating, drinking and talking amidst the background sound of smooth jazz. Everyone was seated in round tables with a few guests squeezing through the room to find a table. The bride and groom, Ashley and Justin had already opened up the wedding reception with the first dance.

"What a beautiful wedding," Sandeep said to Carter.

"Yes, it was," Carter said staring at the bottom of his wine glass.

"Why the long face, Carter. You should be happy for your brother and his new bride."

"I am. But I feel like my brothers are leaving me in the dust with their new brides."

"You're kidding right?" Sandeep said.

"Wrong. I'm not kidding."

"But you have women throwing themselves at you all the time. You could have a bride if you wanted one."

Carter tightened his jaw. "The women I meet are groupies, Sandeep—you know that!" Carter said. "Don't get it twisted. They want my money, nothing else. They could care less about me. I want to meet a nice woman, settle down and have maybe one or two kids."

"I'll bet some nice women are here today," Sandeep said.

Carter felt insulted, Sandeep hadn't listened to a word he'd said. He followed Sandeep's eyes to see what had distracted him and saw a tall slender woman with long black wavy hair, brown shiny eyes, and a wide smile wearing a mint green dress. "What were you saying Sandeep?" Carter mumbled.

"You're babbling, Carter. I can't understand what you're saying," Sandeep said.

"I asked what you were saying," Carter replied, without taking his eyes off of the woman.

"I said, the women here seem nice." Sandeep repeated.

"Yes. I agree," Carter said, his eyes roaming over the woman's shapely figure.

Blessed with a strong attention span, once something caught his attention, Carter became engrossed in what held his interest. In this case it was the woman with the wavy hair in the mint green dress. Carter watched her every move as she walked out onto the balcony to join several women talking, drinking wine and enjoying the view of the vineyard.

When she turned around, Carter made eye contact, giving her his most beguiling smile. She returned his smile. Carter's appreciative eye traveled from her stilettos to her shapely legs to her fitted dress hugging her tiny waist. Carter noticed the woman lower her thick, black lashes when he sized her up.

The band began to play, "I Hear You Calling, by R-Kelly." Carter abruptly ended his conversation with Sandeep and walked over to the woman. He held out his hand. "Would you like to dance?"

The woman followed him onto the dance floor. When Carter took her into his arms to dance, she fit like a glove. "What's your name?" Carter asked through parted lips. He stared at the woman and saw she was more attractive up close.

"My name is Courtney," she said revealing a wide pristine smile.

"What's yours?"

"My name is Carter. So, Miss Courtney, are you related to the bride?" Carter asked looking at her oval shaped face and shiny, expressive eyes.

"Not by blood. I'm her sorority sister. Are you a Greek?"

"No. I didn't pledge when I was in college."

"Any reason?"

"Not really. Just didn't have time."

"I pledged because I wanted to help my community, especially the children."

"Do you have any children?" Carter smiled, glancing at her ring finger.

"I'm raising my nephew Gabriel. Does he count?"

Carter laughed. "Of course Gabriel counts. How old is he?"

"He's six."

"What do you do, Miss Courtney?"

"Call me Courtney," she said as Carter twirled her around. She twirled back into his arms. "I'm a teacher and a freelance graphic artist. What about you? What's your line of work?"

"I'm an engineer."

"Sounds interesting. You like your work?"

"It's okay." Carter changed the subject back to

her. "What grade do you teach?"

"Fourth grade. I used to teach at an elementary school in West Oakland. I'm waiting for them to call me back."

Carter raised his brows. "What made you want to teach?"

"I want to help children learn how to set goals and pursue a higher purpose in life through education."

Carter took a step back. This woman sounded honest and inspiring with a moral compass—a woman of substance. At that moment, for the first time in his life, Carter felt the pierce of Cupid's arrow. Maybe there was help for his heart condition after all. He had to get to know Courtney better.

They danced through several songs, and learned a little about each other until the guests started to leave.

Courtney waved at Melanie and some of her sorority sisters who were leaving. "I guess I better leave."

"May I walk you to your car?"

"Sure."

When they reached her car, Carter said, "I enjoyed dancing with you. Before you leave. Do you mind if I call you?"

"Sure. You can call me." She gave Carter her number while he entered it into his cell phone.

"What are you doing tomorrow?"

"I'm going to visit a couple of wineries before I drive back to Oakland."

"You must be staying the night in the Valley. Where are you staying?"

"I'm staying at the Sutton House."

"Do you mind if I join you on your wine tasting tour tomorrow?"

"I don't date one on one with strangers."

"What if I told you, I'm the bride's brother-in-law? Would I still be a stranger?"

"No. Your relationship with Ashley makes me feel a little easier. Sure, you can come. I was supposed to hang out with one of my sorority sisters, but we decided to reschedule at the last minute."

Carter opened her car door and watched her step inside paying close attention to her shapely legs. "I'll meet you at the country club tomorrow morning at ten." He paused. "If ten is not too early."

"Ten is not too early for me. I'm an early riser."

Courtney closed the door and rolled down her window.

Carter watched as she drove off in her pearl white Lexus sedan.

***

Carter walked back to the winery and met Sandeep coming out.

Sandeep looked at the grin on Carter's face. "Don't tell me. You got her number."

Carter laughed. "I have a date with her tomorrow."

"No way! She's gorgeous. You are one lucky son of a—"

"Yeah, yeah. Don't be jealous, Sandeep. You had the same opportunity to ask her to dance, but you chose to sit and stare."

"I'm happy for you, Carter. "I'll call you on your cell phone if anything jumps off at the office."

"Thanks, my friend."

Carter walked back into the winery and saw Kenton and Brandon sitting in the lounge area by the fireplace. "What's up, Bros?" Carter said as he walked into the lounge with his bowtie hanging loose. He tossed his tuxedo jacket on an empty chair.

"Carter. Did you enjoy the wedding?" Kenton asked.

"Yes. I did."

"What part did you enjoy the most?" Brandon asked.

"The reception."

"I saw you dancing with the woman in the green dress. She looked a little too traditional for my taste." Brandon said.

"She's an interesting woman," Carter said, his eyes sparkling.

Brandon didn't miss Carter's gestures. "Ooh. She has your nose wide open, Bro." He looked at Carter with hooded eyes. "You guys can give up the single life, but not me. I'm never getting married."

Kenton sat up straight leaning forward to hear the conversation. "What's her name, Carter? I saw you dancing with her the entire time."

"Her name is Courtney," Carter said, his face beaming. "All I can say is she's stimulating and intelligent. I was beginning to feel like you and Justin were leaving me in the dust with Briana and Ashley."

Brandon stretched out his arms and yawned. "Both of you are out of your minds."

Kenton gave Carter a look of approval. "Sounds great, Carter. I'm glad to hear you've met someone special."

Brandon began snoring.

"I believe she is a special woman, Kenton."

"Maybe there is hope for your heart condition after all, Brother," Kenton concluded.

***

Carter's limousine arrived at the Sutton House Bed & Breakfast promptly at ten o'clock on Sunday morning. He walked into the lobby and took a seat. He called Courtney on his cell phone.

"Good morning, Courtney. This is Carter. Are you ready?"

"Yeah, give me a minute. I'll be down in a second."

Carter nervously rubbed his hands down his pants leg. He picked up a golf magazine laying on a table next to him. He wanted to spend time alone with Courtney today, but realized he wouldn't be able to ask her any personal questions during the helicopter ride, because the pilot would overhear. He thought about taking her to lunch after the ride, where they would have plenty of privacy. A slow smile crossed his face.

Carter stood up and greeted Courtney with a handsome smile when he saw her walk through the elevator wearing a light blue lambskin jacket, white jeans and a white t-shirt. He scanned her body with approval.

"How are you this morning?" Carter asked.

"I'm fine. Thank you."

"Are you ready to see Napa from above?"

"I can't wait. I wore this jacket in case I get cold in the helicopter."

"Smart thinking. I thought we could go out to taste some wine afterwards."

"Sounds great."

They walked to Carter's waiting limousine and the driver drove them to the Napa Corporate Airport where they boarded the helicopter.

"I've never been on a helicopter before," Courtney said.

"It's a choppy ride, but I think you'll enjoy the experience."

"Why a helicopter?"

"One word. Gridlock. I use a helicopter to get from point A to point B around the Bay Area to avoid getting stuck in traffic."

Once the helicopter took off and they were high in the sky, Carter began pointing out Napa landmarks. "That's the Napa River."

"The river looks like a big question mark from up here."

"See the marina," he said pointing to neatly docked sail boats.

"Look at all of those vineyards. I never knew there were so many."

"My family's vineyard is on top of that hill," Carter said pointing to Underwood Hills Winery. He didn't want to discuss his family with Courtney in front of the pilot.

After they flew around for about an hour with Carter giving her his deluxe tour of the Napa Valley, he said. "Would you like to have lunch with me?"

"I didn't plan to spend much time in Napa today. I have to get back to my nephew. My mother is babysitting him, but she's not well."

"I'm sorry."

"Thanks."

"We can stop at my family's winery and taste some wines. My brother is our vintner, and he recently came out with a selection of white wines.

Would you like to try them?"

"Sure, tasting a few wines shouldn't take all day."

When they arrived at the winery, Carter walked with Courtney into the tasting room where Kenton was serving some wine. "Kenton, this is, Courtney Oliver. Courtney, this is my brother, Kenton."

Kenton reached out and shook Courtney's hand.

Courtney shook his hand. "Pleased to meet you."

Carter nodded his head to Kenton. "I'll take over serving the wine to Courtney."

As if on que, Kenton quietly walked away.

"Courtney, tell me about yourself."

"Well, my life is in transition right now. I'm looking for another teaching job and moving back into my old duplex."

"Where is your duplex?"

"It's over by Mills College."

"I'm sorry, but I don't know the area."

"Mills College is a Women's College that moved to Oakland as a Seminary in 1871."

They tasted wines and talked about their lives until the late afternoon. "It's time for me to leave."

Carter grabbed her hand possessively. "I wish you didn't have to go. Can I come and visit you and Gabriel tomorrow?"

Courtney looked at his hand holding her wrist, and closed her other hand over his. She looked up into his eyes and said, "My house is a mess. I haven't had the chance to unpack."

Carter's hand slid up her arm and back down tightening again around her wrist. "Sounds like you could use a hand."

Courtney blinked her shiny eyes in disbelief. "I couldn't ask you to help me unpack. I only met you yesterday."

"Ask me." Carter smiled a playful grin. "I'm great at unpacking."

Courtney had already paid the movers to place her furniture where she wanted it to go. All she needed to do was unpack boxes in the hall, kitchen and bedroom. "You sure you wouldn't mind?" She scrutinized Carter. He seemed like a trustworthy guy. "Sure. You can come by and help me unpack. But don't be surprised. My neighborhood is nothing like this."

"What time do you want me to come over?"

"The early afternoon. If that's okay."

"I'll come over at noon. Where do you live?" Carter typed her address into his cell phone as she recited it. I must be losing my mind, he thought. He'd never done anything like this before. "I'll take you back to Sutter House to get your car."

Chapter 3

Carter drove Kenton's spare Ford Bronco down Highway 580 in the late morning, exiting on Seminary Avenue. After exiting the freeway, he turned right onto Courtney's street into a working class neighborhood of homes built in the 1950's. He parked in front of Courtney's pink stucco duplex with white trim and walked up the concrete path that led to her front door. Large purple hydrangeas and fuchsia shrubs lined the front of the house on both sides of the path. Walking up two concrete steps, he saw her dainty black mailbox stuffed with mail. He rang her doorbell.

Courtney immediately came to the door wearing black leggings, a white cotton tunic, black strappy sandals and her hair worn upward in a bun. "You made it," she said, her smile reaching her eyes.

"Hello, Courtney." Carter noticed she looked like a model even in her casual clothing. "I'm ready to work."

"Come inside. Let me take your hoodie."

Carter handed her his dark gray hoodie as he stepped over the threshold into the living room and saw a white tile fireplace with a large mirror above it facing him as he stood at the door. A black leather sofa situated under the large front window faced two black leather chairs. Stacked boxes lined the walls of the kitchen, dining room, and hall.

Courtney hung his hoodie in the hall closet. "Thanks for coming. Would you like to sit down?"

"No. I'm ready to work."

"Let's start in the kitchen."

Carter followed her and took a seat at the dining room table. Suddenly he heard footsteps running down the hall.

Six-year-old Gabriel Oliver came into the dining room and stood next to some boxes.

Courtney introduced them. "Gabriel, this is Mr. Underwood. Carter, this is my nephew, Gabriel."

"How do you do Sir?" Gabriel enunciated in perfect English. He held his hand out to shake Carter's.

It was good to see a well-spoken, polite six-year-old, Carter thought. He wasn't used to interacting with children because Jonathan, his only nephew was still a baby. It appeared as though Courtney was doing a good job raising her nephew.

"Gabriel, have you finished unpacking your toys and putting them away?"

"No, I haven't. Can't I talk to Mr. Underwood for a while?"

"Your chores first. When you finish unpacking and putting away your toys in your toy box, then you can come out here with us and maybe I'll order some pizza."

Gabriel's eyes lit up. "Pizza! Yay." He went back into his room and finished unpacking.

"He's adorable," Carter said.

Courtney whispered. "I've had him since he was a baby."

Carter imagined how hard her life must be as a single parent with no one to help her except her sick mother. "It must be hard raising a child by yourself."

"Not at all. It's nice to have someone to greet me at home. Gabriel brings a lot of joy into my life," she said loading the cabinet with a stack of plates and saucers.

Carter saw a large box of pots and pans. "Need some help putting those away?" he said pointing to the box.

"That would be great. They all go in the bottom cabinet next to the stove. If you do that, then I can continue to unpack these dishes."

Carter kneeled down on one knee and removed a large pan out of the box and slid it into the cabinet. One by one he put the pots and pans away until the box was empty. He stood up and helped Courtney remove some dishes from a box on the counter. He came to a crystal trophy in the shape of a triangle with the words 'Miss Oakland' and her name engraved at the bottom. Carter snapped his head around. "You won the Miss Oakland Beauty Contest?"

"Yes. After I'd graduated from high school, I participated in the Miss Oakland contest, and won a scholarship to Sacramento State."

"Where does it go?"

"You can put it on the coffee table in the living room for now."

"So tell me about the pageant. What were your duties?"

"I recorded a public service announcement and gave a presentation to a class of students at Skyline High School. I recorded a short segment on "Mornings on the Bay" which is one of my favorite local TV shows, and I painted a vivid picture of the person underneath the sash and crown."

"What an accomplishment."

"I'm glad you see it is an accomplishment. Most people have misconceptions about beauty pageants. It was important for me to promote the Miss Oakland Scholarship Program and to use my platform to mentor for the organization. It's not all about beauty."

"I can plainly see you're not only a beautiful woman but an intelligent one. Have you ever thought about becoming an entrepreneur?"

"No. I've never thought about that."

"With your graphic arts skills, you could probably learn how to build websites and make a good living."

Courtney cringed at the thought of building a website. She'd taken a computer programming class in college and failed miserably. "I'll give that some thought."

After unpacking all of the kitchen boxes, Courtney offered Carter a bottle of cold water. They sat at the kitchen table. "Do you eat pizza?"

"Yes, I do."

"What kind do you like?"

"I'm not picky."

Courtney picked up her cell phone and ordered a large pepperoni and cheese pizza. It was Gabriel's favorite.

When the pizza delivery man rang the doorbell, Gabriel ran out of his room to the front door.

Carter couldn't help but laugh at Gabriel's

energy. He'd seen nothing but life and love between Courtney and Gabriel in this tiny duplex. He loved it.

Gabriel brought in the pizza and put it on the dining room table.

"Can you handle that pizza? It looks bigger than you." Carter asked. Courtney stood up to pay for the pizza. Carter pressed her shoulder to sit back down in her chair. "I'd like to pay for the pizza since I asked you on the date if you don't mind."

"No. I don't mind. Thank you." Courtney put her money back in her wallet.

"When you ask me on a date, then you can pay," Carter added.

Gabriel grinned at Carter revealing a missing tooth. "I won't drop it." With Courtney's help, Gabriel placed the pizza in the middle of the table.

Carter walked to the door and paid the delivery man, giving him a healthy tip.

Courtney brought in some plates, silverware, and glasses for the cola when she saw Carter pay the delivery man.

Gabriel ran back to his room and came out with his Toy Story Disney storybook.

"Mr. Underwood, would you please read this

story to me. Gabriel pulled a chair next to Carter and handed him the book."

By the time Courtney came back into the dining room, Carter had begun reading "Toy Story," to Gabriel. The scene warmed her heart. Gabriel took to Carter like a bee to honey. "I'm sorry to stop the storytelling, but Gabriel, you need to wash your hands so you can eat."

"Can Mr. Underwood finish the story when I get back?"

Courtney gave Carter an inquisitive look.

Carter gave Courtney a smile that reached his eyes.

"Let's eat first and then we'll talk about that later."

"Reading to Gabriel is fun to me." Carter said smiling.

Gabriel quickly washed his hands and came back to the table and joined Carter and Courtney. There was a buzz of excitement around the table as Courtney slid slices of pizza onto Gabriel's plate. Carter took a slice from the box. Inhaling the pepperoni and cheese reminded him of staying up all night with Sandeep and Reginald eating pizza, studying for final exams and discussing the future of Underwood Technologies. His dream had turned into a time-consuming obsession, forcing him to work twenty-four hours a day, making him an overworked, unhappy man. His initial plan was to get a new perspective on life. Perhaps he was searching for happiness more than anything else. Did he need to travel the world to find happiness? His grandmother had told him sometimes you can find what you're looking for in your own backyard. He had to admit, he was having the time of his life, feeling nothing but happiness eating pizza, reading stories and talking to Courtney in her tiny dining room.

"Mr. Underwood, will you read my story?"

Courtney needed to control her nephew. "Gabriel don't make a nuisance of yourself. Mr. Underwood didn't come over here to read to you."

"It's okay." Carter wiped pepperoni juice from his fingers and picked up the book. "I enjoy reading to Gabriel. Toy Story is a pretty good story."

"You'll be setting a precedent," Courtney warned. He's going to ask you to read to him from now on.

Carter grinned at Courtney's statement. From now on, meant she was open to see him again. That's what he wanted. He continued reading where he left off.

"I love pizza, Mr. Underwood," Gabriel interrupted.

Carter lowered the book. "I love pizza too," Carter added.

"My favorite is pepperoni. What's your favorite kind of pizza Mr. Underwood?"

"Well let's see. I would say pepperoni is my favorite too."

"Yay!" Gabriel raised his arms as if he'd made a touchdown. "I'm glad you didn't say pineapple."

"You don't like pineapple."

"Pineapple is yukky."

"Have you ever tried sausage?"

"Sausage is yukky too."

"What about you, Courtney?"

"My favorite is Combination. I must have my vegetables."

"Vegetables are yukky too."

Carter laughed and turned to Courtney believing he, Courtney and Gabriel could go on like this forever. He bit into a slice of pizza. "Do you guys like sports?"

"We love sports," Courtney said. "We love the Raiders and the Niners."

"I'll have to take you both to some games."

By the time Gabriel finished eating his pizza, he had looked at Carter with hooded eyes, ready to fall asleep. He saw them talking and walked over to the sofa, laid his head down on the sofa and fell asleep.

Carter sat at the dining room table thinking about Courtney's situation. He wanted to make her life easier to raise Gabriel as a single woman but didn't want to offend her. He chose his words carefully. "Courtney, did you get a chance to think about what I said about designing websites? With your skills in graphic arts, you could earn good money designing them."

"I don't know anything about coding."

"I could teach you."

"I don't think so. I'm going to wait until the school calls me back. Until then I'll work temporary jobs designing graphics."

Why don't you let me help you with coding?"

"No thank you. I can handle my career just fine!"

Carter was shocked at Courtney's attitude. His company tutored and trained people every day on all sorts of software. He'd never experienced a woman turn him down for anything he offered, especially his advice which he believed she needed.

His heart opened up to her even more. "I didn't mean to offend you, Courtney. I only wanted to help."

"Thank you for helping me unpack, Carter, but I don't want to learn how to code."

Carter stood up preparing to leave. "When can I see you again, Courtney?"

Courtney walked over to the hall closet and pulled out his hoodie, handing it to him.

"I don't know?"

"Okay. I'll call you tomorrow."

Courtney turned away and closed the door. With a high chin, she trudged into her living room, crossed her arms and sat on her sofa. Who does he think he is trying to force me to learn how to code? I have no interest in the subject. She shifted in her seat. I barely even know the man, and he's already trying to control me, "humph."

Courtney's mother Diane Oliver, a retired teacher and an intellectual snob had raised Courtney to be superior. She cared for both of her daughters, providing mirroring for them, and giving them affection and a sense of value. Courtney felt valued for what she accomplished, for the quality of her performance, not for herself. She believed others loved her only for her success, so she hid her failures. Her pride prevented others from knowing the real person beneath her successful image. Otherwise, she would be rejected. She believed Carter saw right through her façade. Courtney worked hard to please her mother and knew which behavior would produce approving looks and smiles. She connected deeply with her mother as a young child. Her sister did not.

Unfortunately, Courtney's superior attitude hadn't prepared her for failure of any kind. It left her highly vulnerable to the fear of failure she'd internalized deeply. She kept the loss of her house, and her unemployed status a secret from her friends and mother, who was now living on a fixed income and sick. For months, she'd prayed her school would call her back, but it hadn't happened.

She fidgeted on the sofa. If he calls tomorrow, I'm not going to answer his call, she mumbled under her breath. She had pushed Carter away because she feared he would eventually reject her, just like her father had rejected her. It hurt Courtney to her core to know her father didn't want her. He's probably just like Daddy. Then she thought about how kind Carter had been to come over and help her unpack without knowing her. How many people would offer to do something like that? She knew in her heart Carter was a decent guy. Maybe she'd been too hard on him. Perhaps she would give him a chance, if it wasn't too late.

The next morning the phone rang as Courtney unpacked some boxes in her bedroom. It was her school.

Ms. Oliver, this is Mr. Johnson from the Jack London School District calling you back to work."

"When do you want me to return?"

"Can you come back on August first?"

"I sure can."

"I'll send you some paperwork in the mail for you to sign."

"Okay."

August was two months away, and Courtney had plenty of time to put her collapsed life back together. Now that she had her job back, she could keep her house. It could take up to a year to eighteen months for the foreclosure to happen. If she gave the bank some money every month, it would set the foreclosure back even more because they wanted her money, not her house. But she knew she had a bad deal—her house cost more than she could afford. Losing her job and house was a wake-up call for Courtney. She'd learned the hard way that she needed to strengthen her savings to protect her from disaster ever visiting her door again. She needed to prepare to pay for two years of expenses, including her mortgage. She decided to stay in her duplex instead of moving back into her old house while building up her savings account, and investing in a few stocks and bonds and a 401K retirement plan. A smile crossed her face she could not contain. She began to dance in place.

Chapter 4

The morning sun filtered on Carter sitting in his chair by the window in his old bedroom where he grew up at his grandmother's house. He'd gone to sleep late last night feeling a little disappointed over Courtney's reaction to his offer to teach her how to code. He hadn't meant to insult her. He wanted to make her life a little easier. He wondered what kind of woman would reject such an offer. Perhaps it was her pride that made her react that way, or maybe she didn't think she could learn a programming language, or didn't have an interest in building websites.

Whatever her reason, it caused Carter to ask questions about her. What made Courtney tick? More than anything, he wanted to get to know her better. He'd never been this interested in a woman before. Now that he'd met Courtney, he found himself thinking of all kinds of ways to extend his stay in Napa so he could spend time with her.

Carter's brief visit with Courtney and Gabriel had a remarkable effect on him. For the first time in his life, he'd met a woman different from any other woman he'd met before. She was a woman with a moral compass who felt passionate enough about her students to encourage them to reach their highest potential. What an inspiring woman. And his brief experience with Gabriel gave him a glimpse of how life would be as a father. He felt warm and happy spending time with them and helping them unpack. Nevertheless, he still felt disappointed over Courtney's reaction to his offer. Maybe he was moving too fast.

He hadn't thought about Underwood Technologies since he'd met Courtney. Normally, he was consumed with work, building new devices and coding. Now that his time in Napa was coming to an end, he had to admit, he had no desire to go back home anytime soon. No. His heart was on Courtney, and he would do anything to get to know her better.

But what was he going to do about his leave of absence from Underwood Technologies? He hadn't set a date to put Sandeep in charge as CEO. He also had to finish testing his code for his artificial liver.

Fortunately, Carter carried his laptop everywhere he went so he could work on his coding in his down time. He wondered how he could work in Napa and stay in close connection with his office in Silicon Valley. After a second, he snapped his fingers. The winery! He remembered seeing several empty office spaces in the winery. Maybe he could use one of those offices as a satellite office while he stayed in Napa. Not a bad idea. With a satellite office in Napa, he could spend more time with his family and be close enough to get to know Courtney better, if she would give him a chance after he'd obviously insulted her.

He decided to go over to the winery this morning and have a little visit with Kenton and set up one of those vacant offices for himself. He leaned back in his chair and smiled. Problem solved.

Several hours later, Carter walked into the winery with his brown leather laptop bag strapped across his chest. He walked past the gift store, delicatessen and hospitality center, down the hall toward the conference room, where his family met for business meetings to share the annual earnings at the end of the year. The winery was a privately owned partnership between his grandmother and siblings. Carter was glad he'd kept Underwood Technologies privately owned. Sandeep's brother-in-law Sanjay was the Chief Financial Officer and kept track of all new investors.

He stopped at a furnished office next door to Kenton's office. He stuck his head inside of Kenton's office and saw him working on his computer.

"Hey, Bro. Do you mind if I use the office next door?"

Kenton waved his hand, "be my guest, Brother. No one uses it."

"What are you doing?"

"I'm trying to find another manager for our bottling operation."

"What happened?"

"He quit."

"Why?"

"He says our bottling operation is too antiquated and needs to be updated."

"Updated how?"

"Our computers run on antiquated software." He looked up at Carter. "Our software and hardware are obsolete."

"Is it affecting our profits?"

"Yes."

Kenton scanned Carter up and down. "Hey, Brother. You're a computer scientist. I bet you could update our software."

"Sure I could. Need my help?"

"Yeah, but I hate to ask for your help because you've got your hands full running your corporation."

"Bro, this is our family business. Nothing comes before family."

"I'm glad you feel that way, Brother. The winery needs someone with your skills right now. Coders are in high demand. It's almost impossible to find a one with management skills to run a bottling operation."

"You're talking about a major project." Carter paused thinking about the situation. One of his strengths was problem-solving. I'll find a way to update the winery's software and run Underwood Technologies from Napa."

Fortunately, UT was staffed with Sandeep and other competent employees who could run the business while Carter was only a helicopter ride away. "Hey, Brother, I'll do it," Carter said. "Let me know when you want me to start. I've decided to take a leave of absence to travel the world. I'll just make Napa one of my stops. I'll extend my stay in Napa until the software and bottling operation is updated."

Kenton exhaled, and looked up at Carter through strained red eyes. "Thanks, Brother. Your decision saved the winery."

"No problem."

Carter walked into the vacant office and placed his laptop bag on top of the desk. He opened up the plantation shutters to let in some light and pulled out the ergonomic chair from the desk. After taking a seat, he pulled out his cell phone from his pocket and laid it on the pristine cherry desk next to the land telephone.

The first order of business was to call Sandeep

and find out what was going on at UT. He opened his laptop, clicked on his coding software, and then called Sandeep on his cell phone. "What's up Deep?"

"Hey, Carter."

"How's everything going at UT?"

"I have some bad news for you." Sandeep paused for a second. "My brother in law, Sanjay, told me someone has been quietly stockpiling UT shares."

Carter's mouth fell open. "What!" Shocked at Sandeep's statement, Carter began to worry because he originally split the stock three ways between himself, Reginald and Sandeep. He owned forty percent. Sandeep and Reginald owned thirty percent each. Carter never sold any of his stock, so he owned controlling interest in the company. Sandeep and Reginald sold some of their stock to Board members and members of their family. "Do we know who's buying the stock?"

"Sanjay said the buyers are anonymous."

"Who would want to get controlling interest over UT?"

"I don't know? I just wanted to give you a heads up."

"Well, I called to tell you I'll be working from

Napa for a while. I opened up a satellite office at the winery." He looked at the number on the desk phone. "Here let me give you the office landline number, in case you can't reach me on my cell phone."

"I don't think this is a good time for you to be away from the office, Carter," Sandeep warned.

"Why, because someone is stockpiling UT shares?" Carter leaned back in his chair and looked at the vineyard through the window. "Whoever is buying the stock could buy it no matter where I am."

"Touché," Sandeep grumbled.

"Let me know if you hear anything else. In the meantime, I'll hire an investigator to find out who's stockpiling our shares. Carter stated.

"Will do, Carter. How is the coding for the artificial liver coming? You know, Reginald is itching to get it on the market."

"Yeah. I know. I'm in the process of completing the testing today."

"Good. I have a bad feeling about the stock, Carter. I wonder if Reginald is the one buying up the stock."

"Why would you say that? Do you have any evidence?" Carter asked.

"No. Just a hunch."

Carter had overheard Reginald criticizing him to board members before. A few loyal board members had also told Carter that Reginald critiqued Carter for his lack of enthusiasm to develop more lucrative products to increase profits for the corporation.

"Greed affects people in different ways Sandeep." Carter paused. "I hope your hunch doesn't turn out to be true." Carter ended the call and spent the rest of the day testing his code. After working for three hours, straight Carter needed an eye break.

He picked up his cell phone to call Courtney but placed it back on his desk. He decided to back off from Courtney until she cooled down. Besides, who was he kidding? Courtney wasn't interested in him.

***

Later that afternoon, Carter browsed the cable section of the technology store, looking for an external drive, and saw his old high school girlfriend, Brittany Sutton.

"Brittany?" He paused. "Is that you?" Memories of them attending football games and school dances crossed his mind. She was popular and fun in high school, but now that she had matured a bit, she reminded him of her mother.

"Carter. What are you doing here? I thought you

lived in Silicon Valley."

"I'm home helping my family with some technical issues at the winery."

"What have you been doing lately? Are you still working as a Wedding Planner?

"Don't you know? I planned your brother's wedding."

"No, I didn't know."

"Um hum. I've been working like a crazy person lately. Everyone wants a Napa Valley wedding these days."

Carter chuckled. "You did a great job on Justin's wedding."

Brittany was the last young lady Carter dated. As his high school sweetheart, he remembered them having a sort of puppy love, barely kissing. He always thought Brittany was a nice girl, but it was her mother he disliked. Victoria Sutton tried to force them into a serious relationship before they graduated from high school, but Carter had a problem with her mother forcing him into a relationship. He couldn't imagine having Mrs. Sutton as his mother-in-law, so he ended his friendship with Brittany. As always, he liked Brittany as a friend. But now, Courtney held a special place in his heart.

Several weeks had passed since Courtney had heard from Carter. She wondered why he hadn't called her back like he promised. He'd just fallen off the radar. Maybe it was because how nasty she treated him over the coding issue. She decided to call Ashley, now that she was a member of Carter's family and find out if she'd heard anything. She called Ashley on her cell phone.

"Ashley, this is Courtney."

"Hi, Courtney! How are you?"

"I'm okay. Where are you?"

"I'm still on my honeymoon sailing around the world, but we're coming back home early."

"Why?"

"Because, I've been suffering from seasickness."

"I'm sorry Ash. If this is a bad time I can wait until you get home."

"Please. This is not a bad time. We're staying in a hotel in Argentina, Justin is asleep right now. What's up?"

"Well, I was wondering if Justin has talked to Carter lately."

"Yes, he talked to Carter the other night."

"Oh?"

"Um hum. Carter told Justin he was staying in Napa so he could update some winery software. He also told Justin he ran into his old high school flame, Brittany Sutton."

"Sutton, that name sounds familiar."

"Brittany's parents own Sutton House."

"That's it! I stayed at Sutton House Bed and Breakfast, the day before your wedding. Tell me more about Brittany."

"All I know is she's one of the hottest wedding planners in Napa Valley. She planned my wedding. If you stayed at Sutton House, then you must have met her mother."

"Victoria? Yes, I met her. She's very professional and nice."

"Well, what's going on with Brittany and Carter?"

"Before I get into that, tell me what happening between you and Carter? Justin told me Carter thinks you're not interested in him."

"I can't blame him for thinking that way. I messed up Ash, by pushing him away."

"You need to get him back because Carter is a good man."

"From what I can tell, I think you're right. Tell me more about Carter and Brittany. Are they getting serious again?"

"I don't think so, but who knows. Justin told me Carter always thought Brittany was a nice girl, but he can't stand her mother."

"Why?"

"Because she tried to force them to get married right out of high school. If you know Carter, you know he hates to be forced to do anything. He told Justin he couldn't imagine having Victoria Sutton as a mother in law."

"Oh, my."

"What kind of person is Brittany? Is she nice?"

"Justin told me she's a bit controlling but nice."

"What if Carter gets serious about her? What am I going to do Ash?"

"Have you called Carter to express some interest in him?"

"No."

"Then maybe you should call him and apologize for whatever you did to push him away."

"I'll call him. Have you taken something for your seasickness?"

"Yes. It's getting better, but we're still coming home early."

"Try to enjoy your honeymoon anyway Ash."

"I will. How's Gabriel and your Mom?"

"They're fine. Gabriel took to Carter like a magnet."

"Sounds like you have feelings for Carter too."

"Yes, I do. I just realized how much after talking to you. Goodbye, Ashley."

"Goodbye, Courtney."

***

Early in the morning, Carter picked up his cell phone and saw he'd missed Courtney's call. He immediately returned her call. "Hello, Courtney, I'm returning your call."

"It's good hearing your voice, Carter," Courtney said.

"I'm glad you called. I thought you were angry at me."

"I'm not angry at you, Carter. It was all a misunderstanding. I have to be honest with you, Carter, I failed a computer programming class when I was in college. I was too proud to tell you that coding is not my forte. I called to apologize for treating you so badly when you left. Now I realize, you were only trying to help me."

"Yes, I was trying to help you. Apology accepted." Carter smiled. "I enjoyed spending time with you and Gabriel."

"Me too. Thanks again for your help. Gabriel asks about you every day."

"Would you and Gabriel, like to join me for lunch today?"

"Sure. But first, I have some good news."

"Tell me."

"My school called me back to work."

"Good for you. We have something to celebrate today."

"Yes. I'm pretty happy."

"Where are we going for lunch?" Courtney asked.

"Since it's such a warm sunny day outside, why don't I pick up some sandwiches here at the delicatessen, and we can eat them at Lake Anza in the Oakland Hills."

"What a good idea. I'll get Gabriel ready. We'll both be ready by the time you get here."

"Okay, see you soon." Carter smiled as he ended the call.

***

A little past noon, Carter picked up Courtney and Gabriel. As he drove on the highway leading to the East Bay hills, the scenery changed from crowded urban housing to thick groves of Redwood trees. After about thirty minutes, he took the Lake Anza Road exit and noticed the area looked like a different world. Carter parked in the parking lot near the Tilden Regional Park Lake Anza sign.

Gabriel was the first one to jump out of the car from his Spiderman booster seat. He snatched some water toys and handed Carter a beach ball he'd blown up.

"Hey, Buddy, slow down and wait for us," Carter said coming around to open Courtney's door.

After freshening her lipstick in the visor mirror, Courtney gave Gabriel a serious look, "Slow down, Gabe. You know better."

"Okay. I'll wait." After pausing a minute, Gabriel grabbed Carter's hand, "come on Mr. Underwood. You're too slow."

Carter started laughing, "Let me get the picnic basket. You want to eat lunch don't you?"

"Yeah. I'm hungry."

"Well then hold on."

Courtney grabbed Gabriel's hand, and held the beach ball, while Carter opened the trunk, pulling out a picnic basket full of goodies and a blanket. They all strolled down the boardwalk until they reached the white sand beach. Carter laid down the blanket on top of the sand with Courtney's help. After sitting down, Carter opened up the picnic basket full of sandwiches, pickles, fruit, bottled water, soft drinks, a couple of wine glasses and two bottles of Underwood Hills wine.

Carter looked out into the lake, reflecting the azure sky. "This lake is beautiful. Not many people here today."

"It's like this all the time except for the weekends." Lowering her head, she said, "I used to bring Gabriel here when we lived in my old house. It's not too far from here," Courtney said looking out into the lake.

Carter didn't miss Courtney's gesture as he handed her some sandwiches. She probably feels embarrassed about losing her house.

Courtney unwrapped a sandwich and handed it to Gabriel along with a bottle of juice while Carter uncorked a bottle of white wine. Gabriel scarfed the sandwich down getting mayonnaise all over his face.

"Here, Gabriel. Take this napkin and wipe your

face. You act like I don't feed you."

After spotting a few children, Gabriel asked, "can I go in the water and play now?"

"You know the rules. Only on the shore. You know not to go in the water unless I'm in there with you especially after eating."

"I know, Auntie."

Gabriel took his beach ball and ran out to greet the children playing on the shore.

Carter leaned back on one elbow and took a bite of his sandwich. "Want some wine?"

"Whew. I need some dealing with Gabriel."

"Is white okay?"

"Sure, since I'm eating a crab sandwich."

Carter poured a little white wine into two glasses and handed one to her. After they had finished their sandwiches, Carter munched on some grapes and thought about a scene he'd seen in a movie. He held a small bunch of grapes up to Courtney's mouth and said. "Take a bite."

Courtney laughed. "What is this? Do you think I'm a Roman Empress or something?"

"No. I'm just a man crazy about you," Carter said in a self-confident voice. His glance slid rapidly to her bathing suit he could see beneath her sheer cover-up and his mouth softened.

Courtney tried to throttle the dizzying current racing through her from the wine or was it from Carter's closeness. She could feel Carter's magnetism by the way he looked at her. He kissed her slowly and gently, as light as the summer breeze blowing on her face from the lake.

Courtney heard Gabriel's voice as he played with a little boy he'd met. "He'll be out there all day if I let him."

"Let him play. I want to spend more time with you. We can keep an eye on him from here."

Suddenly Courtney's cell phone rang. It was her real estate agent.

"I need you to take a look at some offers for your house. Can you come by your house today around five o'clock? I'm showing it to some people around six."

"Sure. I can meet you there at five."

***

Courtney arrived at her Oakland Hills home fifteen minutes early to meet the real estate agent. She leaned on the For Sale sign in front of her house, feeling relieved to hear she had received some offers. All kinds of thoughts raced through her mind, mainly regret.

Courtney led Carter and Gabriel up the pathway leading to the house. The real estate lady had not arrived yet. Fortunately, Courtney had her spare key to open the door. When they walked inside, Gabriel immediately ran to his old room.

Carter walked into the living room with maple hardwood floors, a large fireplace, cathedral ceilings and floor to ceiling windows that looked out into a million dollar view of the San Francisco Bay. "Nice house, Courtney. Too bad you're selling it."

"Yeah. I wish I could have kept it, but I just couldn't afford it after I was laid off for so long."

"You want to give me a tour while we wait."

"Sure. Why not."

"This is the formal dining room," Courtney said. She slid her hand across the cherry dining table. "All of the furniture is staged."

They walked through the dining room into the kitchen. "This is the kitchen," Courtney said remembering all of the meals she and Gabriel ate in the breakfast nook overlooking a perfectly trimmed lawn in the backyard. They walked upstairs and came to the spacious master bedroom with maple hardwood flooring, white plantation shutters, and an adjacent bathroom with marble floors. A large white octagon whirlpool tub and steam shower, surrounded by marble, were the main attraction. Then they walked down the hall to Gabriel's bathroom where they heard sobs.

They walked into Gabriel's bedroom and saw him sitting in the middle of the floor with his legs crossed.

"What's the matter, Gabriel?" Courtney asked.

"I miss my room," He said between sobs.

Carter's heart sank at the sight of Gabriel's crocodile tears. He couldn't stand to see children cry or suffer in any way, no matter how trivial.

"I know, Baby. Auntie misses her room too. But you have a new room."

"My new room is not the same," He said sniffling.

"Come here, Baby. Let me hold you." She sat on the floor with him and held him in her arms like she did when he was an infant. "Everything's going to be okay, Gabriel."

The scene almost brought tears to Carter's eyes. Spending time with Courtney and Gabriel taught him the true meaning of family. His heart had softened because he saw himself in Gabriel. Watching Gabriel cry brought back memories of how he felt growing up with a house full of brothers. He felt crowded out, believing they only tolerated him because he was too young, so he withdrew into his world of computers. But then one day, he'd heard them saying, that's just Carter being himself, but we love him anyway—that's our Bro! Since that day, he always addressed his brothers as Bros.

Courtney looked at Carter staring at her while she held Gabriel. "Changing schools and neighborhoods has been rough on Gabriel. He was beginning to act out after the move, but fortunately, I was able to help him through his heartbreak, until now."

Carter looked at Courtney and decided he had to help them. It would cost nothing for him to buy this house. He had to find a way to get Gabriel's room back for him.

The real estate lady walked through the front door. "Courtney? Are you here?"

Courtney dried Gabriel's tears with the tail of her cover-up and told him to stay in the room. She and Carter walked downstairs to meet the real estate agent.

"Hello, Regina." She introduced them. "Carter, this is Regina Wright, my real estate agent. Regina, this is Carter Underwood, a good friend."

Carter shook Regina's hand.

"Here is the list of six offers I've received so far," Regina said handing the list to Courtney.

"Wow, six offers already? You're doing a great job, Regina."

"I have a couple coming over to see the house at six."

"Do you have a business card, Ms. Wright?" Carter asked.

"Sure do." She pulled out a card from her wallet and handed it to Carter.

Courtney was too busy looking at the offers to notice Carter taking Regina's card.

"I like the third offer," Courtney said. "It's the highest, and it's for cash."

"I'll let the couple coming by today know they must exceed that offer."

"Okay. We're moving on."

"Carter, do you mind going to get Gabriel?"

"Sure." He walked upstairs and saw Gabriel still sitting in the middle of the room. "Come on, Gabriel. It's time to go."

Gabriel looked up into Carter's face with sad eyes. Carter wiped Gabriel's eyes with his thumbs. There was no way Carter was going to let anything keep Gabriel from getting his room back. Carter had a plan.

Chapter 5

Carter tapped his fingers on his desk as he sat in his office thinking about Gabriel. He pulled out Ms. Wright's business card and called her. She didn't answer, so he left a voice mail message indicating he wanted to bid ten percent over the highest offer for Courtney's house, and would pay cash, with the stipulation he remain an anonymous bidder.

He turned around to face his computer and began correcting error messages for his software. After testing the software, it came back with no errors. He clapped his hands loudly.

Standing up, he walked over to the window and stretched. He rested his foot on the window sill as memories of his kiss with Courtney crossed his mind. A flock of blackbirds flew over the vineyard below as his mind burned with thoughts of Courtney. He'd never felt this way about a woman before. He didn't know why thoughts of her distracted him. Normally, when he was working, wired into the zone, nothing distracted him. But now that he'd met Courtney, distractions and time weren't so important to him anymore.

His loved spending time with Courtney and Gabriel. His mind drifted to images of Gabriel handing him that Toy Story book to read. He'd never known he could be so affected by a child. He loved the way Gabriel pulled his hand, trying to get him to go into Lake Anza. A smile crossed his face as he remembered the incident. He loved sitting on the beach sharing grapes and wine and kissing Courtney.

What was he going to do about Courtney's pride? On the one hand, he loved her for being too proud to let him teach her coding, but then, on the other hand, he knew her life was hard raising Gabriel as a single woman.

Their lives contrasted, she lived in a tiny duplex, and he lived in a sprawling mansion in Hillsborough, a city full of wealthy neighbors. He wondered how she would react if she saw his mansion? Would she think they were unsuitable because they had nothing in common? And how could he ask her to put the brakes on her issues with pride, when he had issues with withdrawal? No. They both had flaws, and he had to find a way to prevent their flaws from ruining their future happiness. He was determined to work on his.

Carter stuck his head inside Kenton's office. "Hey, Bro. Let's take a walk around the warehouse. It's been a long time since I've been inside. I can barely remember what it looks like."

Elated that Carter had decided to help him, Kenton pushed back his chair and stood up. "I'll be glad to walk with you."

Carter followed Kenton through the tasting

room, down the stairs to the cellar and through the back door of the warehouse. As they walked through the warehouse, Kenton reminded Carter of the process for bottling wine. Carter had walked through the warehouse with his family many times as a teen. He remembered watching wine pour into the bottles before traveling on the conveyor belt to the area that pushed corks into the neck of the bottle.

"Okay, I remember this machine. It pushes corks into the bottle on the conveyor belt, but what happens next?" Carter asked.

"The bottle is sealed to ensure the cork won't explode off in transit." Kenton said, pointing to the machine.

"Where is the computer stored to run this equipment?"

"In that room over there." Kenton said, pointing to a room the size of his office. They walked into the computer room.

Carter took a seat in front of an antiquated terminal in the temperature controlled room. He opened up some files and said, "I can't believe we are running the bottling operation off of this obsolete hardware and software written in this old computer language."

"You're speaking Greek to me," Kenton said standing over Carter's shoulder.

"We need to switch to an open language."

"Well, you're the expert, Carter. How long do you think it will take for you to develop the new software?"

"No telling. I'm committed to this project for as long as it takes." Carter saw curious employees glancing at him now and then through the window. He stayed in the computer room, evaluating the software until Kenton turned to leave.

Kenton slapped Carter on the back. "Well, I'll leave you to your computers, Brother. Thanks again for helping."

"No problem, Bro." Carter said typing on the keyboard as he slowly became wired into the zone. After several hours, Carter made a list of the new computer equipment the bottling operation would need.

Carter returned to his office and called his technology vendor where he purchased computers for Underwood Technologies and ordered a new system for the winery.

After he had hung up with the vendor, Carter called Courtney. She answered her phone.

"Courtney, how's your day going?"

"Gabriel and I just came back from the park."

"Hey listen. Would you and Gabriel, like to join me for dinner tonight? I know of a great Chinese restaurant."

"Well, I don't think so. Gabriel is real picky. He doesn't like Chinese food, but thanks for the offer. Why don't you come over here for dinner? I'm making Gabriel's favorite, spaghetti and meatballs."

"Spaghetti sounds great. I love Italian food. What time should I come by?"

"We usually eat around five or six o'clock."

"I'll be there around five thirty." Carter hung up the phone and closed his laptop. He stuck his head into Kenton's office and saw he'd left. Probably out in the vineyards.

***

Carter stood in front of his mirror tucking the tail of his light blue cotton polo shirt inside his khaki trousers. He wasn't one for what he and his colleagues called getting suited up. He preferred dressing casually every chance he got. After patting a spicy aftershave on his cheeks, he walked down the hall and saw his grandmother sitting in her bedroom.

"Where are you going, Carter?" Henrietta said, closing her Bible.

"I was invited out to dinner?"

"Oh?" She smiled, waiting for him to tell her more.

He was about to walk down the stairs but remembered he hadn't seen his grandmother all day. He walked into her room and kissed her on the cheek. "My friend, Courtney invited me over for dinner."

"Who's Courtney?" Henrietta said looking up at Carter through her inquisitive eyes. "I don't mean to pry—but tell me about her."

"I'm running late. I don't have time to talk now, Granny, but I'll tell you about her later." He kissed her again. "I love you, Granny."

"Okay, Grandson. I'll see you later."

Henrietta went back to reading her bible in her chair by the window. Carter zipped down the stairs and jumped into his car.

***

Once Carter arrived at Courtney's house, he saw flashing lights coming from two police cars and an ambulance down the street. He drove down further and saw an old man leaning on a cane on his front lawn.

Carter rolled his window down and leaned over the passenger seat. "What happened?" Carter asked.

"Drive by," the old man stated nonchalantly.

"Does this sort of thing happen very often around here?"

Throwing up his hands, the man sighed. "Almost every day." He shook his head. "Gangs killin' each other over turf," the old man said before turning around to go back inside.

"Gangs," Carter mumbled. The old man's words chilled Carter to his bones. He worried about Courtney and Gabriel's safety living in this neighborhood. He was glad he planned to buy Courtney's old house. He had to get them out of this neighborhood.

Carter drove back to Courtney's house and rang the doorbell. He heard Gabriel's little feet racing toward the door.

Gabriel swung the door open and greeted Carter with a bright, cheery face. "Hi, Mr. Underwood!" Gabriel said taking Carter by the hand. Auntie is making spaghetti for dinner tonight.

"Ooh. I can't wait," Carter laughed as Gabriel drug him into the kitchen. He got a kick out of Gabriel's enthusiastic little attitude.

"Hi."

"Hi, yourself." Courtney said to Carter, as she stirred the sauce in the large saucepan.

Carter walked over to her standing over the stove and kissed her on her neck.

"Did you hear the police cars?"

"Yes, I did. Have a seat."

"There was a shooting down the street."

"There are always shootings down there."

"Don't you care?"

"Of course I care, but there's nothing I can do. How did your day go?"

Carter could tell she didn't want to talk about the crime in her neighborhood, so he decided to save the conversation for a later time. He changed the subject. Need any help?"

"Do you know how to make a salad?"

"No, I don't. But, I'm willing to learn. Just tell me what to do."

She pointed to the refrigerator. "Pull the lettuce, tomatoes and cucumbers out of the vegetable bin."

"Shouldn't I wash my hands first?"

"Yes you can wash them right over there," she pointed to the kitchen sink.

Carter walked over to the sink and picked up a

bar of soap she had by the knob and began washing his hands. This was the first time Carter came close to cooking anything. He pulled the ingredients out of the refrigerator and brought them over to the counter where he saw a cutting board.

"All you have to do is pull each leaf off of the head of lettuce and let it run under the water."

"I want to help!" Gabriel said watching Carter place the ingredients on the cutting board."

Carter looked at Courtney. "Can he help me?"

"Sure. You can pull each leaf off and let him run it under the water." Courtney said placing a salad bowl next to Carter. She looked at Gabriel. "Make sure you wash your hands first."

Gabriel drug up a chair to the sink and kneeled on it.

Carter handed him the soap. "Here use this, Buddy." Carter felt entertained and delighted cooking with Courtney and Gabriel.

Gabriel smiled with a huge grin on his face while washing his hands.

Carter tore off a lettuce leaf and handed it to Gabriel.

Gabriel held each leaf under the running water until it was clean and then placed it into the salad bowl. "So what did you do today, Gabriel?"

"I went to the park and climbed on the lion statue and swung on the swings and slid on the slide while Auntie read a book."

"That sounds fun." After Carter had finished, he watched Gabriel playing in the water with the last leaf. "So Courtney, what did you do today?"

"Nothing, other than take Gabriel to the park and prepare to start back to work. August is right around the corner."

"What about you. What did you do today?"

"I decided to help my family's winery by updating the bottling operation."

"You're amazing. But when are you going back to your company in Silicon Valley?"

"I'm not going back anytime soon."

"Why not?"

"Because my family needs me more right now. Underwood Technologies has people capable of running the company while I'm away."

"That's great." Courtney walked over to the sink and poured the large pot of boiling spaghetti into a colander. After draining the spaghetti, she put it in a large pasta bowl and then carried it to the dining room.

Carter crossed his arms as he leaned against the dining room table. "That looks so good."

Gabriel crossed his arms as he stood next to Carter. "Yeah. It looks good, Auntie." Gabriel looked at Courtney and asked, "Auntie, can we look at Ratatouille tonight?"

"Sure you can look at it after we eat."

"Can I put it in now?"

"Go ahead."

Now that Carter and Courtney had some time alone, Carter walked behind her and kissed her. "I've wanted to do this since I walked through the door."

Courtney turned around, "Me too."

"Oh no!" Courtney said, pushing away from Carter. She turned off the fire in time before the sauce boiled over. She poured the sauce and meatballs into a large bowl and placed it on the table.

"Why don't you pull out some plates from the cabinet? You remember where the plates are, don't you?"

"Yes, I believe we put them in this cabinet," Carter said opening the cabinet door. He pulled out three plates and began placing them on the table.

His heart felt warm and content spending time preparing a meal with Courtney and Gabriel. He found some glasses above the plates and placed three of them on the table too.

"There is a cold pitcher of lemonade in the refrigerator," Courtney said as she finished the salad.

Carter pulled the lemonade out of the refrigerator and placed it on the table. He looked in the drawers for the silverware and placed forks, knives and spoons by each plate. He took a seat on the side of the table and watched as Courtney brought the salad to the table.

"Dinner's ready Gabriel!" Courtney said.

Gabriel paused his movie and ran to the table. "I'm starving, Auntie."

Courtney sat at the head of the table, and Carter sat at the other end.

After they all had taken their seats, Courtney asked, "Carter would you like to do the honor of blessing the table?"

Carter repeated the blessing he remembered hearing his father give when he was a boy. Carter never felt so good in his life having dinner with Courtney and Gabriel.

"Mr. Underwood, have you ever seen

Ratatouille?"

"No. I haven't, and now that I know you better, you don't have to call me Mr. Underwood anymore."

"What should I call you?"

"Let's ask your Auntie."

Courtney looked up from her plate. "Gabriel, why don't you call Mr. Underwood, Uncle Carter?"

"Okay. Uncle Carter. Do you want me to tell you about Ratatouille?"

"You will spoil the movie if you tell me," Carter said, twirling some spaghetti around on his spoon with his fork.

"You're right. I'll wait." Gabriel observed Carter twirling his spaghetti around on his spoon, and tried to do the same, but it didn't work. "I can't twirl my spaghetti like you Uncle Carter."

Carter stood up and walked over to Gabriel, he took his little hands into his large hands and showed him how to twirl his spaghetti on a spoon. "See, this is how you do it."

Gabriel stuffed his mouth with the spaghetti on his fork.

Carter sat back down and turned to Courtney. "You're a good cook, Courtney. This is the best

84

spaghetti and meatballs I've ever tasted."

"Gabriel, why don't you help clear the table," Carter offered.

Courtney snapped her head to Carter. "Please don't give orders to my nephew. That's my job."

Carter leaned back in his chair. "I meant no harm."

"None was taken." Courtney said. "Gabriel is too small to carry glass dishes. He might break one and hurt himself."

"I hadn't thought about that."

"It's okay."

Carter realized Courtney was not a push over. He stood there analyzing her for a moment. She appeared to be an inner-directed woman who spoke her mind. Maybe she was used to giving instructions and didn't like people telling her what to do because of her occupation. He noticed how protective she was of Gabriel, which was fine with him, because he liked strong, capable women.

"Gabriel, go back in the living room and look at your movie." Courtney ordered.

Gabriel obeyed his aunt and turned around from the dining room table, and went back to his movie.

"Would you like me to scrape the plates?"

Carter offered with a smile.

"Sure, scrape everything into the garbage disposal and I'll load the dishes in the dishwasher."

Carter scraped each dish into the garbage disposal before handing it to Courtney. This was all new to Carter, and he loved it.

"Want some popcorn to go with the movie?"

"Sounds great," Carter said.

Minutes later, they all settled in the living room to watch Ratatouille. Carter sat on the sofa and wrapped his arm around Courtney's shoulders while Gabriel found a spot on the floor right in front of the television. When the movie came on, Carter laughed and snorted on the funny parts.

Gabriel looked up and saw Carter wiggling his eyebrows at him. "This is my favorite part." Gabriel jumped up and started singing a song from the movie.

Carter listened to the words as Gabriel sang the song holding his arms out. After Gabriel had finished the song, he sat back down and once again became completely engrossed in the movie.

Warmth spread throughout Carter's body as he rubbed Courtney's shoulder while they watched the movie. He made a mental imprint of how happy he felt this moment in time. Carter couldn't remember ever feeling this happy. After catching a glimpse of life with Courtney and Gabriel, his heart had completely changed from being a self-centered CEO to a happy, smiling man for the first time in his life.

Chapter 6

Henrietta Underwood looked up from her newspaper. She still subscribed to the Napa Register newspaper even though Carter had given her a tablet for Christmas.

"Morning, Granny."

"Morning, Baby Boy." Henrietta never let any of her grandsons know she called them all Baby Boy in private. She called Carter Baby Boy because he was her second youngest grandson who had a tendency to isolate himself when he was growing up. Back then she brought him back into her world, with her chocolate chip cookies. But now he was a man, living on his own, coming back home for holidays. "How did your date go last night Carter?"

Carter poured himself a cup of coffee. "It went great, Granny." He poured some cream and sprinkled some sugar into his coffee. "She prepared spaghetti and meatballs. Her six-year-old nephew, Gabriel and I made the salad."

"How was it?"

"It was the best spaghetti and meatballs I've ever tasted." He sat in the chair next to her. "You never cooked spaghetti and meatballs for us when we were growing up, Granny."

"No honey. Your granddaddy didn't like Italian food--he was a die-hard Texan, who loved his meat and potatoes."

"So tell me about this girl, Carter."

"Well, Granny, she was laid off from her job for six months that led to her losing her house and moving back into her old duplex she'd been renting out."

"I'm sorry to hear that. What kind of work does she do?"

"She's an amazing fourth-grade teacher who inspires her students to set goals. Fortunately, the school district called her the other day to come back to work in August."

"August is just around the corner."

"I know. She's raising her six-year-old nephew, Gabriel by herself."

"Why is she raising her nephew?"

"Because his mother is on drugs."

"Oh, my."

"I offered to help her earn extra income by teaching her how to write code and build websites."

"What did she say?"

"She wasn't interested."

"Why do you think she refused your help?"

"I'm not sure—maybe pride. I know she could do it because she's a smart capable woman. We met at Justin's wedding, so I don't know her very well. What I do know about her now, is she's a die-hard teacher who feels passionate about her students. I'm attracted to her because she's honest, intelligent and inspires her students to set goals to pursue a higher purpose in life. She's also gorgeous. She won the Miss Oakland Beauty Pageant."

"She sounds like a nice girl, but don't overlook her issue with pride. I'll tell you why. Pride can be positive or negative. Pride is what made your granddaddy resist sharecropping in Texas and come to California during the Great Migration looking for a better life—and look what we found. Yet, pride can be a destructive force. Look how your father's male pride ended his marriage to your mother. She left because he was too proud to have a working wife. He held her back from becoming a lawyer, which was something she wanted to do badly."

"I know why Mama left us, Granny. But, Courtney's pride not only hurts her but others too. She's raising her six-year-old nephew in a high crime neighborhood running the risk of him becoming another statistic."

"You should encourage her to move."

"And have her reject me again. She's not the kind of woman you can control by telling her what to do. Anyway, Granny, I didn't come down to have coffee with you to talk about Courtney. I came because I want to talk to you about some personal issues I'm facing."

"What's that, Baby Boy?"

"Love."

Henrietta smiled while she stirred another Splenda into her coffee. "What do you know about love? You've never brought a woman home and introduced her to the family before."

"You're exactly right, Granny. I know nothing about love. Kenton told me I had a heart condition that needed an overhaul or tune up."

Henrietta laughed. "An overhaul. Kenton is a mess." Then she paused for a second and gave Carter a serious look. "You're telling me you've never been in love?"

"Never. Granny, I spend all of my time inventing medical devices to help people instead of doing what I need to do to help myself find love and happiness." He gave his grandmother a pained expression. "Courtney makes me feel happy by doing simple things."

A wide grin crossed Henrietta's face. Now she could stop worrying about Carter. "Baby Boy, if this girl makes you happy, then you should keep seeing her. Why spend all of your time working if it's not making you happy. Don't other people know how to make those machines? If this girl makes you happy, then you should follow your heart, and spend time getting to know her."

"Thanks, Granny. It's nice talking to you again." He paused. "I forgot to tell you I'll be staying in Napa for a while longer to help Kenton upgrade the software for the winery's bottling operation."

Henrietta lowered her head and looked up at Carter above the rims of her bifocals. "Um hum. Bottling operation eh?"

Carter started laughing. "What's with the um hum?"

"I think you want to stay in Napa so you can court—what's her name again?" You know I'm bad with names."

"Courtney. Her name is Courtney."

"You're partially right, Granny, but Kenton asked me to help him out at the winery. So I'm taking a leave of absence from my company to work here at the winery for a while. Besides, Sandeep is taking over my duties, and there are lots of employees who can run the everyday business operation while I'm away." He gulped the last of his coffee. "Goodbye, Granny." He kissed her on the cheek. "I need to work in the winery today. I'll see you later."

Hours later Carter called Courtney.

"Hey, Courtney, I had a great time last night with you and Gabriel. I'm calling to see if you and Gabriel would like to take in a San Francisco Giants baseball game with me on Thursday?"

"Sounds great Carter. I think Gabriel would love to see a live baseball game. He was so happy when the Giants won the World Series."

"Okay. I'll pick you two up on Thursday."

***

As Carter crossed the Bay Bridge, Gabriel marveled at everything he saw. He pointed to Alcatraz Island. "What's that Auntie?"

"It's called Alcatraz Island. There's a prison on the island." Courtney felt guilty for never bringing Gabriel to San Francisco.

"Prison?"

"Yes. But the prison is closed now." She looked at Carter. "That's where the Birdman of Alcatraz served time."

"The Birdman of Alcatraz? Auntie, will you tell me the story of the Birdman?"

"I'll tell you about him one day." Courtney saw Carter take the third street exit. "Right now we're going to focus on going to the baseball game."

Carter pulled up to the AT&T Ballpark.

"Who is that, Uncle Carter?" Gabriel said pointing to a bronze statue of a baseball player swinging a baseball bat.

"That's Willie Mays."

"Who's he?"

"He was a famous baseball player for the San Francisco Giants a long time ago before you were born."

Carter parked in a permit-only parking lot and opened the car doors for Courtney and Gabriel. They all followed an usher to the Underwood Technologies private suite where Carter entered with Courtney and Gabriel. Carter stood with them at the door, listening to the voices come to a complete silence.

Carter knew many of his employees knew very little about his personal life. They knew he spent days and nights in his office, had an imaginative mind, and hated interruptions. He scanned the room, watching his employees stare at him standing at the threshold with Courtney and Gabriel, knowing they stared because they'd never seen Carter with a woman or a child.

Carter strode into the room in unison with Courtney and Gabriel and greeted Sandeep.

"Glad you made it Carter," Sandeep said remembering Courtney from the wedding.

"I'd like to introduce you to Courtney Oliver and Gabriel, her nephew."

"Pleased to meet you," Sandeep said holding out his hand to Courtney. "I remember you from the wedding," Sandeep said giving Courtney a mesmerizing smile.

"Nice meeting you."

Carter watched as Reginald Ainsworth approached him.

"I haven't had the pleasure of meeting your beautiful guest, Carter," Reginald said glancing down at Gabriel.

"Courtney, this is Reginald Ainsworth, the Marketing Director of Underwood Technologies."

"Pleased to meet you, Mr. Ainsworth," Courtney said politely.

After the introductions, caterers brought in lunch for everyone.

Carter turned to Courtney. "Are you hungry?"

"Thanks, but not right now." Courtney nodded

her head in the negative.

"What about you, Gabriel?" Carter asked.

"Yeah, I'm hungry."

"Let's get a hot dog." Carter turned to Courtney. "Can you find our seats, Courtney?"

Courtney found their seats.

When Carter and Gabriel returned with hot dogs and drinks, Gabriel jumped into the seat next to Courtney. Carter reluctantly sat next to Reginald.

"Did you complete the software to operate the artificial liver?" Reginald asked.

"It's finished. I emailed the program to Sandeep yesterday."

"I've put together a great marketing plan for the artificial liver."

Carter didn't respond to Reginald's babblings. He didn't come here to talk about business. He came there to see the game. Carter turned his back to Reginald and faced Gabriel for the rest of the game. He told Gabriel everything happening with each player who came up to bat.

"The catcher is catching a great game today, Carter said to Gabriel."

"Yeah. He's my favorite player. We only get to

see baseball on television at home."

"Aren't you glad you came out here today?"

"Yes, I am, Uncle Carter." Gabriel grinned with mustard all over his mouth that Courtney did not see. Carter took a napkin and wiped Gabriel's mouth.

Reginald did not miss a single action. "When are you going to take your leave of absence?" Reginald asked.

Carter regretted not sending an email to the entire staff informing them of his leave of absence. "I'm on leave now, Reginald." Carter stated in an irritated voice.

"So when did you meet your beautiful friend?" Reginald asked.

"Why do you need to know that, Reginald?" Carter was getting upset with Reginald's annoying questions.

"Well because there's something different about you. You look like, like—a family man. Who knew you'd get involved with a ready-made family."

"What did you say?" Carter felt like hauling off and slugging Reginald for the slight.

"Come on Reginald, let's get a drink." Sandeep said, sitting on the other side of Reginald.

Carter's nose flared with anger when they both walked away.

Courtney and Gabriel hadn't heard the slight.

Carter stood up and marched toward Sandeep and Reginald. He wanted to fire Reginald on the spot, but he couldn't because Reginald held an elected office as the Chairman of the Board for Underwood Technologies and the board had to vote him out of office.

Carter walked up to Reginald and spoke in a hardened voice. "Don't you ever say anything about my relationship with Courtney ever again, or else you'll find yourself knocked out on the floor."

Sandeep's eyes widened at the threat.

Reginald took a step back and gulped with a dry throat.

Carter went back to Courtney and Gabriel. Hours later, the game ended. The Giants had won the game. "Come on, let's go," Carter said to Courtney and Gabriel.

They all turned around and left as quietly as they came.

On the way back home, Carter felt guilty because he had not been honest with Courtney and Gabriel about where he lived. He had to come clean and let them know he lived in a 25,000 square foot, home in the exclusive San Francisco Peninsula neighborhood of Hillsborough where only millionaires lived. He hoped they wouldn't withdraw from him if he showed them his house.

"Hey you guys, would you like to take a trip to my house down on the Peninsula tomorrow? I need to pick up some important papers."

"Sure. Why not Courtney said. I don't have any plans for tomorrow." Courtney turned around and saw Gabriel had fallen asleep with remnants of dry mustard all over the front of his shirt. "I don't think Gabriel would mind. You know, he loves you, Carter."

Carter smiled.

***

The next morning, Carter picked up Courtney and Gabriel and drove them up the circular driveway to his Hillsborough mansion.

Courtney got out of the car and started laughing. "You're kidding aren't you?"

"No. This is where I live."

Gabriel had fallen asleep during the long ride. He rubbed his eyes upon awakening and beamed with happiness. "This is your house, Uncle Carter?"

"Yes. It is," Carter said looking at Courtney

sideways.

Courtney returned his look. "I didn't know it would be so…so…"

"Big." Carter said finishing her sentence. "I just wanted to be transparent with you Courtney. Would you like a tour?"

"Yeah." Gabriel jumped out of the car and ran up to the front door. "There are two lions on each side of the door, Auntie, just like the lion statue in the park.

Courtney remained silent.

Carter took her by the hand. "Come on. Let's go inside."

As they walked around touring the house, Carter felt Courtney pull her hand away from his. "So what do you think?"

"I think this house is beautiful but overwhelming. I couldn't imagine cleaning all of this," she said looking around.

"You wouldn't have to--there are maids." He looked at her and grinned.

Courtney grinned back. They both stood there having a moment.

Gabriel looked at them, "why are you and Uncle Carter looking at each other so silly?"

Courtney and Carter burst into laughter.

Courtney crossed her eyes at Gabriel and said. "Because we're silly people."

Gabriel grinned at them. After Carter had shown Courtney and Gabriel his house and retrieved his documents, Courtney asked him a question. "Why did you choose to go into your own business rather than work in your family's winery?"

"I didn't have a talent for winemaking like my oldest brother." Carter said. "My talent is in technology."

"So you said you're an engineer?"

"Yes. I'm a bioengineer."

"You own your company, right? I saw the sign Underwood Technologies in the suite at AT&T Park."

"Yes. I am the CEO of Underwood Technologies."

"CEO? As in owner?"

"Yes. What are you thinking?"

"I'm thinking you are an obviously talented, accomplished man." Courtney paused for a moment. "Why didn't you tell me about all of this before?"

"I'm telling you now."

Courtney crossed her arms.

"You have to understand Courtney. I lead a very private life."

"I understand. I have my issues with privacy, and you have yours."

"I have issues?" Courtney said.

"Yeah." Carter replied.

"What are my issues?" Courtney asked.

"I think you might have a slight issue with pride." Carter said.

"Pride?"

"Yes."

"Why would you say that?"

"Because you'd rather raise Gabriel in a high crime neighborhood, risking him becoming another statistic rather than allowing me to teach you how to write code to build websites and increase your income."

Courtney dropped her chin. "I—I'm not good with computers."

"Coding isn't hard. You could earn extra

income from building websites and purchase your old home from me."

"What do you mean? Purchase my old home from you? I sold my old home."

"I bought it. It's one of the many properties I own all over the Bay Area."

"You bought my house?"

"Yes. It's there waiting for you and Gabriel to move back in."

"But why?"

"I want Gabriel to get his old room back. Don't get me wrong. I love your duplex. It's warm, cozy and comfortable. But it's located in a high crime area." He observed her reaction, hoping she wouldn't become angry. "You can pay your mortgage to me every month, and I'll help you and Gabriel move back in if you want me to."

Courtney put her ego on hold and thought about Carter's offer. He had a way of making her feel naked by removing a cloak she'd hidden under for as long as she could remember. She internalized Carter's argument and admitted her old neighborhood had changed for the worse since she'd lived there. She knew she was putting Gabriel at risk by living there, but she didn't like being in debt.

"Could you lower the payments to an affordable level?"

"I see no problem with that. You've been through hell and high water, and you need to let me help you."

"Thank you, Carter. And yes, I would love for you to help us move back into our old house. So how much are you going to charge me for the mortgage payment?"

Carter thought about the drive-by incident. "You can pay what you can, when you can, until you get back on your feet."

Courtney looked around the huge house. "So are you going to continue to live way out here?"

"No. It's too far from my family and too much house for me. I purchased it as an investment. I'm planning to sell it now that I'll be working full time in my family's winery."

A smile crossed Courtney's face. "You're going to work full time at your family's winery?"

"Yes." Carter took her smile as a green light for a kiss. He pulled her into his embrace and gave her a slow drugging kiss that sent the pit of her stomach into a wild swirl.

Chapter 7

At midnight, Carter walked up the dark staircase and passed his grandmother fast asleep in her room. He walked down the hall to his room and plopped onto his bed. He stared at a poster of Einstein, his high school idol, still hanging on the wall. Now that he'd revealed his true self to Courtney, he felt relieved. He was happy Courtney hadn't felt insulted when he told her he'd purchased her house. He was also happy she'd taken his advice about not raising Gabriel in a high crime neighborhood. Her attitude proved she was dealing with her pride.

He was dealing with his trust issues because for the first time in his life--he trusted Courtney and her adorable nephew. Both of them changed his life and his heart. For the first time in his life, he didn't think only of himself. He wanted to help others— specifically, Courtney and Gabriel.

He wanted to deepen his relationship with Courtney. Maybe he could take her on a vacation to his condo in Hawaii before she started back to work. That was it! He'd ask her tomorrow if she wanted to join him on a weekend getaway to Hawaii.

The next morning, Carter called Courtney.

"Good morning beautiful."

"Hi, Carter."

"I have a question for you?"

"What?"

"Ever been to Hawaii?"

"Hawaii. No. I haven't."

"Would you like to go?"

"Yeah. I'd love to go, but not with you."

"Why not?"

"I haven't known you long enough."

"How long do you need?"

"I don't know, Carter. It will take some time because we're only "dating." We're not going together. I'm not even your girlfriend."

"Then what are you?"

"I'm your friend."

"Let me ask you this, Friend. If I were one of your sorority sisters, would you go to Hawaii with me?"

"Yes. I mean—I don't know what I mean."

"Why don't you pretend I'm one of your sorority sisters and come with me to Hawaii?"

"I'm not going to sleep with you, Carter."

"That's okay. I'm not asking you to sleep with me." He gave her mischievous look. "I'm offering you a chance to take a short vacation before you go back to work," he said holding up his palms.

"Who's going to watch Gabriel?"

"What about your mom?"

"She's been keeping him a lot lately. I don't want to abuse her help. I would go if I could take Gabriel."

Carter stared at Courtney. "Do you think you might be a bit over-focused on Gabriel? You need to balance your life instead of smothering Gabriel."

"What do you mean, smothering Gabriel?"

"You smother him, Courtney. Give the boy some space."

Courtney's mother had told her the same thing-- she smothered Gabriel. She thought about adding some balance in her life. Against her better judgment, she decided to go to Hawaii. "Okay, maybe I do smother Gabriel, but it's because I keep having dreams of my sister taking him back and ruining his life. I just want to protect Gabriel."

"I understand, Courtney. But unless your sister is completely clean of drugs, she'll have to fight both of us in court if she ever decides to take Gabriel back."

"We could bring Gabriel with us since it's a short weekend getaway."

"I do need a break, and if it's only for the weekend?" She paused for a moment, running her fingers through her hair. "Maybe I could ask my mother to keep Gabriel for the weekend. What weekend were you thinking about going?"

"Any weekend is good for me."

"Let me call my mother and see when she can watch Gabriel. I'll let you know what she says."

"Okay." Carter walked over to open the blinds and looked out at the vineyard thinking about his kiss with Courtney. "I'll be waiting for your call."

***

One week had passed, and it was mid-day when Courtney looked out the window of Carter's private jet and saw the green island of Oahu. Before she was laid off, Courtney and Gabriel took a summer vacation every year. Now that her life was back to normal, she knew she better enjoy this trip before the start of the school year.

Courtney was glad she wore a sleeveless marine

blue short dress when she disembarked the airplane into the warm island air. Carter wore a Hawaiian shirt and khaki shorts. Everywhere Courtney looked she saw lush vegetation, brilliant exotic fragrant king-size flowers attracting butterflies and birds. The fragrant air made her feel as if she were visiting another world. Fortunately, Carter had a jeep waiting at the Kalaeloa John Rodgers Field Airport.

Carter felt consumed with the heady effect of Hawaii. He opened the car door for Courtney. "Come on beautiful," he said while throwing their luggage in the back seat. "Let's go to my condo."

They drove down the freeway lined with wild hot pink Bougainvillea vines. They stopped at his luxurious high-rise condominium on Ala Wai Boulevard surrounded with palm trees.

"This is beautiful."

"Hello, Mr. Underwood," a valet said, opening Courtney's car door.

Carter looked at his badge and greeted the valet.

Courtney watched the valet put their luggage on a cart as they entered the lobby.

"You have a valet here?"

"Come on let me show you around." He gave her a tour of the first floor. When they came to the elevator, Carter pushed the button to the twenty-first floor. Carter opened the door to his condominium surrounded by floor to ceiling window all with views of the Pacific Ocean.

All Courtney saw was blue sky and water when she walked into the living room. She walked through the sliding glass door leading to the elegant terrace. "Look at this view." She turned around and saw the heart-rending tenderness of his gaze. "This is beautiful."

"Not as beautiful as you," he said looking her over seductively. His gaze dropped from her eyes to her shoulders to her breasts.

She noticed he was watching her intently. "Are you going to give me a tour," she said looking up at him through thick lashes.

He took her slender hand into his own while they walked into the kitchen. "This is the kitchen."

Courtney walked into the kitchen and slid her hand across the cool marble countertop. "Nice kitchen." Leaning against the dark wood paneling covering the refrigerator, she asked. "How often do you come here?"

He stepped up closer to her. The prolonged anticipation of kissing her was almost unbearable. "Once, maybe twice a year." He casually leaned his large hand against the wood paneling and took her hand into his other hand. He leaned in and kissed her as softly as a Hawaiian breeze. His tongue sent shivers of desire racing through Courtney's body. After the long, languid kiss, he raised his mouth from her and gazed into her eyes. "Want to see the bedroom."

Courtney's eyes had a burning faraway look in them. Her lips were still warm and moist from his kiss. She nodded her head.

Carter took her by the hand and led her into the large airy bedroom decorated in a neutral color scheme with a king size bed covered with a white cotton coverlet accented with sand colored pillows. "This is a nice big comfortable looking bed."

Carter knew if he didn't put their bags in the bedroom right now, they would never get there. He went into the living room and rolled in their bags. "Are you tired? Do you want to relax before I show you around the island?"

"No. I am anything but tired."

"Let's unpack and I'll drive you around the island. Then we'll come back and have dinner at my favorite Japanese restaurant."

***

Carter drove Courtney around the sunny side of the island showing her Diamond Head Mountain, the sandy Waikiki beach, Iolani Palace, home of Hawaiian royalty, and the Hawaiian Cultural Center and other major landmarks. He ended the tour with a drive on the dusky side of the island with a cooler ecosystem. After the tour, they stopped at his favorite Japanese restaurant located in a Hawaiian Village.

The hostess led them to a table in a secluded corner and pulled out Courtney's chair. As soon as they sat down, a waitress took their order. When the waitress left, Carter took Courtney's hand and said, "I have something to ask you, Courtney."

"What do you want to know?"

Carter pulled out a small box from his pants pocket. "You can tell by now that I have strong feelings for you, Courtney."

Courtney gasped. Leaning back in her chair, she covered her open mouth with her hands.

"Courtney, I fell for you the moment I saw you at my brother's wedding. You've captivated me, and I want you to be your woman." He opened up the box displaying a brilliant two carat solitaire ring. "Courtney, will you be my woman and wear this ring to represent my feelings for you?"

Tears glistened in Courtney's eyes. "I'm attracted to you, Carter, but I'm not interested in a serious relationship right now because I'm so focused on building a life for Gabriel."

"Remember what I told you before we left?"

"What?"

"You shouldn't smother Gabriel."

"Yes, I remember."

"Please promise me you will find some balance in your life, Courtney instead of over protecting Gabriel."

Courtney knew Carter could see through her like glass. She had to admit Carter had proven that he had Gabriel's best interest at heart which meant so much to her. "Okay, Carter. I'll be your woman."

Carter took the ring out of the case and slipped it on Courtney's left hand, third finger.

Holding her arm out, she looked at the ring and then at Carter. "It's beautiful."

"Not more beautiful than you." Carter's eyes were as soft as a caress. He kissed her hand and filled her glass with wine. "I'd like to propose a toast" he paused. "Nothing but happiness for my woman."

Courtney smiled. "Nothing but happiness for my man."

***

Carter kissed Courtney on the ride to the twenty-first floor only stopping when the doors opened. The walked down the hall hand in hand until they got to Carter's condominium. Upon entering, Carter swept her weightless, into his arms and walked into the bedroom. Courtney buried her face against his throat and put her arms around his neck. Her soft curves molded to the contours of his lean body. His mouth covered hers hungrily leaving her mouth burning with fire. Gently, he eased her down onto the bed and unbuttoned her blouse. He undressed her slowly, worshipfully discarding her clothes before removing his shirt and trousers. She lay naked beneath is gaze as he stood above her in all of his masculine glory. He slid next to her, his lips touching her nipple with a tantalizing possessiveness. Her breasts surged at the intimacy of his touch. His hands massaged her hips and thighs. His gentle massage sent currents of desire through her. His hands searched for a pleasure point that he found as Courtney moaned at his magic touch. His body imprisoned hers in a web of growing arousal. She gasped as he lowered his body over hers crushing her breasts against the hardness of his body. "Am I too heavy?"

She breathed in a deep soul-drenching breath and shamelessly said, "no Carter. Don't stop."

That was all Carter needed to hear before he moved his hands downward, skimming either side of her body to her thighs. She snuggled against him as their legs were intertwined. They moved together as one taking the time to explore, arouse, and give each other pleasure. Passion pounded the blood through Courtney's heart, chest, and head. Love flowed into her like warm wild honey that she welcomed into her body. Carter's expert touch sent her to a higher level of ecstasy. Together they found their tempo until they reached the peak of delight that exploded in a downpour of fiery sensations. Courtney gasped in sweet agony and then drowned in a floodtide of the release of her mind and body.

Carter reclaimed her lips and crushed her into his embrace where they slept entwined all night long.

***

The next morning Carter brought two cups of coffee into the bedroom. He sat on the side of the bed looking at Courtney as she lay sleeping in all of her beauty. He knew Courtney was the woman for him. He'd always wanted to find the right woman and settle down and have a family, but his billionaire status prevented him from meeting the right woman. He even thought of hiring a matchmaking service to find the right woman.

Before he'd met Courtney, when he needed a date to take to an event, he paid one of the gold-digging groupies who hung around Silicon Valley parties and social events, but getting involved with those women, may have been convenient, but always turned into a complication.

What was it about Courtney that drew him to her like metal to a magnet? He had to admit her beauty first attracted him. After he'd met her at his brother's wedding, eaten meals at her house, finding out she was a good cook and saw how devoted she was to her nephew, he realized he trusted her. Trust? Where did that come from, she thought? Where ever it came from, he knew in his gut she was one woman he could trust.

Before he met Courtney, he determined the woman he married would have to sign an iron-clad prenuptial agreement. But now, all of that had changed. Like his grandmother said— he would find the right woman someday, and he would know her when he saw her.

He knew in his heart he wanted to marry Courtney, but he didn't want to ask her to sign a prenuptial. He'd talked to his brothers about this subject before. Kenton was against prenuptials. Brandon was for them, and Justin had no comment—just the legal facts. Right now he was determined to enjoy his weekend with Courtney, but she was sleeping it away. He wanted to wake her up and take her to Waikiki Beach for a swim.

He leaned over to her and kissed her softly on her cheek. He whispered her name into her ear.

Courtney lifted one lazy eye and then the other until Carter's handsome face came into focus.

"Morning beautiful."

"Good morning to you too Mister." She smiled at him while stretching her arms. "I have to tell you something."

"What's that?" Carter said nibbling at her ear.

"Last night was wonderful."

"What a nice thing to say."

"Last night felt good to me too, Courtney."

"I have a nickname for you, Carter."

Carter laughed. "What name is that?"

"Lover Man."

Carter threw back his head and let out a loud laugh. "Lover Man, that's a new one for me. No one's ever called me that before."

Joy shone in Courtney's eyes. "You know you're a good lover."

"I have a lot more of that for you, Baby."

Courtney lay her head on Carter's lap. "I never want to leave Hawaii."

Carter leaned down and gave her a slow, thoughtful kiss. "I wanted to take you to Waikiki Beach this morning, but I don't think we're going to make it." His hand moved to skim her hips and thighs while he kissed the buds of her swollen nipples. His gentle massage sent currents of desire through her once again. He removed his pajama bottoms and slid under the sheet and made sweet love to her over and over all day long.

Later that afternoon they woke up and showered together. Carter washed her shoulders kissing them seductively.

"You see there, Carter. That's why I call you Lover man."

"You can call me that all you want beautiful."

"I'll reserve that nickname for when you and I are alone."

"That's fine with me," he said, pressing her against the marble wall. He lifted her up into his arms. She wrapped her thighs around him as the warm water showered on their bodies. They moved until they found their tempo, their bodies in exquisite harmony with each other, soaring higher until waves of ecstasy throbbed through them. Her body melted against his, and her world filled once again with Carter. She knew Carter was the one man on earth she could ever love.

When they finished their shower, they dressed in their bathing suits and drove to the beach.

Carter spread out his towel and then hers. They both sat down waiting for the sunset. Carter leaned back on an elbow and looked up at the dusky sky. He pulled Courtney into his embrace.

"I love you, Courtney."

"I love you too Carter. You fit in perfectly with

my little family. Gabriel loves you more than you know."

"I suspected that." He kissed her long and seductively as the golden Hawaiian sun slowly sank into the Pacific Ocean.

Chapter 8

At midnight, Carter pulled the sheet away from his body and walked through the sliding doors onto the terrace to feel the cool Hawaiian breeze. He looked up at the large silver moon and inhaled the fragrant foliage as he leaned over the terrace thinking about his life. He turned his head around when he heard Courtney's footsteps.

Walking into his embrace, Courtney said, "It's warm tonight."

"Yes. I couldn't sleep."

"What are you thinking about?"

He rubbed her bare shoulder. "My family."

"Tell me about your life growing up in Napa."

Carter pulled her into his embrace and spoke into her ear. "My parents divorced when I was a toddler. My mother left when I was a baby, so I never got to know her. All of my life, I've wanted to develop a relationship with her, but my father forbade it. When he died, I was busy in college and never took time out to cultivate a relationship with my mother. When she died last year, I felt like life had knocked the air out of me. I recently decided to take a leave of absence from my company." He

120

rubbed the tips of his fingers along Courtney's back. "To get back to your question, I lived in a house full of brothers when I was growing up. As a younger brother—nothing I could do was wanted or needed by my father or older brothers, so I looked for something I could bring to the table. I looked for areas of expertise my brothers had not already explored. I found my gift in the field of technology, and majored in biomedical engineering when I went to college." He released her from his embrace and leaned on the bannister. "When I was in my senior year at Stanford University, I invented a medical device that detects heart blockage, and then became very wealthy."

Courtney leaned over the bannister and looked into the silver disk in the Hawaiian sky as she listened to Carter. "I'm sorry you felt ignored by your family, but I bet they are proud of you now."

"Yes, they are." Carter felt embarrassed talking about his adolescent feelings when he was growing up. He changed the subject to focus on Courtney. "What about you Courtney. How was your life growing up?"

"When I was growing up, I was valued for what I accomplished. My mother valued me for the quality of my performance in school, but not for myself. I believed she and others would love me only for my success. I was afraid if people got to know me, they would see I was an imperfect person and reject me. I sought out help for my problem. My therapist says I have a fragile self-image I'm trying to protect. She warned me that preserving my self-image would come at a great cost to my happiness. So you are not by yourself, Carter. I have my issues too."

Carter's heart sank hearing the sadness in Courtney's voice. He thought he had problems with his mother. He empathized with her feeling valued for her performance, and not herself. "What about your father?"

"I never knew my father. I've always believed if he didn't love me enough to be in my life, then how could other people, love me just as I am."

Carter pulled her into his embrace. "It seems as if we both need each other to help deal with our childhood issues. I don't want you to feel you have to perform to make me happy. You make me happy by simply being you. I love you just as you are Courtney with all of your imperfections. I hope you love me despite mine."

"I do."

"Come on, let's go back to bed."

***

Sunday morning, Carter and Courtney boarded the chartered airplane bound for Napa where his driver was to meet them. The weekend had passed much too quickly for Carter. He felt like a schoolboy in love for the first time in his life.

As days passed, Carter couldn't get Courtney out of his mind. Normally he would be wired into the zone coding with great intensity, with no thoughts of what he used to call romantic distractions. But now all he could think about was Courtney. He saw her face everywhere he went. He couldn't eat or sleep. So this is how it feels to be in love, he thought. It was a new experience that left his mind swirling in circles. He hurled back to earth as reality struck in the sound of Kenton's voice.

"Carter...Carter."

Startled, Carter looked up from his computer screen and saw Kenton standing in his doorway. He cleared his thoughts. "What's up, Bro?"

"I came in to talk to you."

Carter gestured for him to sit down in one of the leather tufted chairs in front of his desk. "What do you want to talk about?"

"I need to talk about the winery."

"I saw they delivered the new computers and servers the other day. How's the software development going?"

"It's about fifty percent complete. I'll begin testing next week."

"Good, but my concern is about other areas of the winery." Kenton clutched his arm.

"What areas?"

"Mainly our Internet and mail-order sales need to increase to cover the cost of new state regulations. We also need new labels for our white wines I'll be placing on the market. We also need an attorney who can help us get around these new regulations regarding water usage and the drought."

"Wait a minute. You've been handling all of these problems by yourself, in addition to your winemaking activities?"

"Yes, Brother. Since the bottling manager retired, some of the weaknesses in our winery are coming into clear focus."

"What do you suggest?" Carter asked

"That's what I came to ask you. I thought we need to add more people to the winery's payroll."

Carter observed Kenton's concerns with extraordinary perception and insight. "I think we need to call a family meeting."

"A family meeting."

"Yes. It's time for the family to pitch in and help the winery deal with some of these problems."

"How can the family help?"

"Brandon is a classically trained artist. Why can't he design the labels for our new line of white wines?" Carter became engrossed in the solutions to these problems. "Justin is a highly trained attorney. Why isn't he representing the winery? We shouldn't have to pay outside attorneys to and handle new state regulations." When it came to his baby sister, he displayed remarkable intelligence and foresight. "Although Crystal is still in college, she has something to offer."

"Crystal is training to be a veterinarian, what can she possibly bring to the table?"

"She can handle the Internet sales and the mail-order business. She's always had great entrepreneurial skills running one internet business after another. She can handle this one. We don't need to add more people to the winery's payroll. We need to get the family to kick in and help."

"You've single-handedly solved the problem of the day, Brother. When should we call the meeting?"

"There's no need to wait. Let's call it for Sunday after we have dinner with Granny."

"That's a good idea."

Carter stood up and patted Kenton on the shoulder. "Don't worry, Bro."

Late Sunday afternoon Carter, Kenton, Justin, Brandon and Crystal sat around Henrietta's dining room table.

Carter made the announcement to the family that the winery needed help in all of the areas he and Kenton had discussed. "Kenton is the only one working in the winery right now. I've joined the winery to help update the bottling operation. We need the rest of you to pitch in."

"Why does the family need our help?" Justin asked.

Carter looked at Justin in the eye. "You are an attorney at law. There is no reason the winery should pay an outside law firm to handle our legal matters. The winery needs you, Justin, to represent us in legal matters."

"But I'm a Civil Rights lawyer. I can't represent the winery in court."

Carter gave Justin a frustrated look. "Yes, you can." He turned his attention to Brandon scrolling through his cell phone. "Brandon?"

"Huh?" Brandon didn't look up at Carter.

"Brandon. The winery needs you to design some labels for our new line of white wines."

"Labels? I'm a painter, not a graphic artist. But I can do that. When do you need them?"

"We will let you know. Why don't you start working on the labels and show us a few designs within the next two weeks."

"No problem."

"Thanks, Bro." Carter looked at Crystal playing with her unseasoned meal Ruby had prepared. "Crystal."

Crystal looked up from her plate. "Huh?"

"We need you to pitch in too."

"What do you want me to do?"

"We want you to work the weekends and handle our Internet mail-order and wine club sales."

"I can care for the horses in the stables, and take the Internet mail-orders and wine club sales."

"Kenton will go over the details with you," Carter said standing up, "now I'll ask the question." Carter looked around the table. "Raise your hand if you can pitch in and help the winery."

"What's the worst case scenario if we don't pitch in?" Justin asked.

Brandon looked up from his cell phone to hear the answer to Justin's question. "The winery will lose money, and there will be fewer profits to split between us at the end of the year."

"I'm in," Brandon said, raising his hand.

One by one, the rest of them raised their hands.

Kenton stood up and gave Carter a hug whispering in his ear. "You did it, Brother. You've saved the winery."

Carter beamed with pride and love at Kenton's statement.

"That's all I've ever wanted to do, Bro."

"Are ya'll finished?" Henrietta said. Everyone nodded their heads. "Then the family meeting is over. Let's have coffee in the living room."

As everyone sat in the living room talking and catching up on what was happening in each other's lives. Henrietta suddenly grabbed her chest and slumped over in her wheelchair.

Briana saw it first and ran to Henrietta's side. "Kenton, call 911." Granny-Nana is sick. Everyone surrounded Henrietta.

Brandon called 911 on his cell phone. "I just called Briana."

Crystal's medical training kicked in. She took control of the emergency and gave directions. "Kenton and Justin lay Granny down on the floor." Crystal began administering CPR to Henrietta.

The first responders arrived within five minutes

and took over. They took Henrietta to Queen of the Valley hospital. Crystal's CPR had saved Henrietta's life. They all went to the hospital and waited to hear from her doctor. Carter called Courtney from the waiting room.

The doctor came in later and informed the family that Henrietta had suffered a heart attack, but would be fine. Courtney and Gabriel arrived an hour later to support Carter. Courtney told Carter she was staying with him. She asked Ashley if Gabriel could spend the night at her house. Ashley picked up a sleepy Gabriel and took him to her house to spend the night. Carter asked the nurse if she could set up two beds in Henrietta's private room. The nurse agreed. "Mainly our Internet and mail-order sales need to increase to cover the cost of new state regulations. We also need new labels for our white wines that I'll be placing on the market. We also need an attorney who can help us get around these new regulations regarding water usage and the drought."

"Wait a minute. You've been handling all of these problems by yourself, in addition to your winemaking activities?"

"Yes, Brother. Since the bottling manager retired, some of the weaknesses in our winery are coming into clear focus."

"What do you suggest?" Carter asked

"That's what I came to ask you. I was thinking

we need to add more people to the winery's payroll."

Carter observed Kenton's concerns with extraordinary perception and insight. "I think we need to call a family meeting."

"A family meeting."

"Yes. It's time for the family to pitch in and earn some of those profits we all share at the end of each year, and help the winery deal with some of these problems."

"How can the family help?"

"Brandon is a classically trained artist. Why can't he design the labels for our new line of white wines?" Carter became engrossed in the solutions to these problems. "Justin is a highly trained attorney. Why isn't he representing the winery? We shouldn't have to pay outside attorneys to and handle new state regulations." When it came to his baby sister, he displayed remarkable intelligence and foresight. "Although Crystal is still in college, she has something to offer."

"Crystal is training to be a veterinarian, what can she possibly bring to the table?"

"She can handle the Internet sales and the mail-order business. She's always had great entrepreneurial skills running one internet business after another. She can handle this one. We don't need to add more people to the winery's payroll, we need to get the family to kick in and help."

"You've single handedly solved the problem of the day, Brother. When should we call the meeting?"

"There's no need to wait. Let's call it for Sunday after we have dinner with Granny."

"That's a good idea."

Carter stood up and patted Kenton on the shoulder. "Don't worry, Bro."

***

Late Sunday afternoon Carter, Kenton, Justin, Brandon and Crystal sat around Henrietta's dining room table.

Carter made the announcement to the family that the winery needed help in all of the areas the he and Kenton had discussed. "Kenton is the only one working in the winery right now. I've joined the winery to help update the bottling operation. We need the rest of you to pitch in."

"Why does the family need our help?" Justin asked.

Carter looked at Justin in the eye. "You are an attorney at law. There is no reason why the winery should pay an outside law firm to handle our legal matters. The winery need you Justin to represent us in legal matters."

"But I'm a Civil Rights lawyer. I can't represent the winery in court."

Carter gave Justin a frustrated look. "Yes you can." He turned his attention to Brandon scrolling through his cell phone. "Brandon?"

"Huh?" Brandon didn't look up at Carter.

"Brandon. The winery needs you to design some labels for our new line of white wines."

"Labels? I'm a painter, not a graphic artist. But I can do that. When do you need them?"

"We will let you know. Why don't you start working on the labels and show us a few designs within the next two weeks."

"No problem."

"Thanks, Bro." Carter looked at Crystal playing with her unseasoned meal Ruby had prepared. "Crystal."

Crystal looked up from her plate. "Huh?"

"We need you to pitch in too."

"What do you want me to do?"

"We want you to work the weekends and handle

our Internet mail-order and wine club sales."

"I can care for the horses in the stables, and take the Internet mail-orders and wine club sales."

"Kenton will go over the details with you," Carter said standing up, "now I'll ask the question." Carter looked around the table. "Raise your hand if you can pitch in and help the winery."

"What's the worst case scenario if we don't pitch in?" Justin asked.

Brandon looked up from his cell phone to hear the answer to Justin's question. "The winery will lose money and there will be less profits to split between us at the end of the year."

"I'm in," Brandon said, raising his hand.

One by one, the rest of them raised their hands.

Kenton stood up and gave Carter a hug whispering in his ear. "You did it, Brother. You've saved the winery."

Carter beamed with pride and love at Kenton's statement.

"That's all I've ever wanted to do, Bro."

"Are ya'll finished?" Henrietta said. Everyone nodded their heads. "Then the family meeting is over. Let's have coffee in the living room."

As everyone sat in the living room talking and catching up on what was happening in each other's lives. Henrietta suddenly grabbed her chest and slumped over in her wheel chair.

Briana saw Henrietta first and ran to her side. "Kenton, call 911." Granny-Nana is sick. Everyone surrounded Henrietta.

Brandon called 911 on his cell phone. "I just called Briana."

Crystal's medical training kicked in. She took control of the emergency and gave directions. "Kenton and Justin lay Granny down on the floor." Crystal began administering CPR to Henrietta.

The first responders arrived within five minutes and took over. They took Henrietta to Queen of the Valley hospital. Crystal's CPR had saved Henrietta's life. They all went to the hospital and waited to hear from her doctor. Carter called Courtney from the waiting room.

The doctor came in later and informed the family that Henrietta had suffered a heart attack, but would be fine. Courtney and Gabriel arrived an hour later to support Carter. Courtney told Carter she was staying with him. She asked Ashley if Gabriel could spend the night at her house. Ashley picked up a sleepy Gabriel and took him to her house to spend the night. Carter asked the nurse if she could set up two beds in Henrietta's private room. The nurse agreed.

Chapter 9

It was August, and the leaves were beginning to change colors. Courtney's luck had changed thanks to Carter helping her with her new mortgage and opening her eyes to the risk of raising Gabriel in a high crime neighborhood. Carter was right, her destructive pride had caused her to hide the truth about losing her house from her mother. She'd even stooped to the level of bribing Gabriel with a trip to Disneyland, to keep the move back into the flatlands a secret from her mother. But, now she was back at work and living in her old house in the hills. Courtney happily sat her old desk at Martin Luther King Elementary School, checking her emails on her laptop. Her goal was to do her best to ensure she would never get laid off again.

She opened an email from the school principal asking her to take the lead in coordinating the Christmas party for the after school program. She looked at another email from the district office informing her the students enrolled in her after school program had all passed the national standardized test.

"Maybe that's why they called me back," she said softly. Courtney had worked hard to raise her student's reading, writing, and math skills at or above grade level. Despite the heavy cutbacks in the budget, apparently the school district appreciated her efforts enough to call her back to work.

Courtney had chosen to teach under-performing students at MLK School because most of the students came from neighborhoods nicknamed the killing zone. She wanted to help her students pull themselves out of that environment with a good education. Courtney inspired them to set and accomplish goals.

Courtney grew up with a natural beauty her sister Kendra did not possess. When they were growing up, Kendra was the oldest daughter and resented that Courtney took her good looks after her mother's side of the family. Kendra looked like their father's side of the family. She eventually dropped out of high school and started hanging out with the wrong crowd. After Courtney won the "Miss Oakland." beauty pageant and won a scholarship to attend Sacramento State University, Kendra spiraled into a dark life of drug abuse. By the time Courtney graduated from college and had established herself at MLK School, Kendra had become pregnant with Gabriel.

Kendra had no idea who had fathered Gabriel. She stayed with their mother until Gabriel was born. The hospital called CPS when they saw Gabriel was born addicted to drugs. Instead of giving Gabriel up to CPS, Courtney, and her mother agreed to raise Gabriel together, even though her mother, a chain smoker, had recently retired due to Lung Cancer.

Their mother, Diane Oliver, had tried all of her

life to work with Kendra's low self-esteem, but she came to the conclusion that she had one good daughter and one bad daughter, and began to treat them differently. Courtney patterned herself after her successful mother, a Professor of Humanities at the University of California. Dr. Oliver educated herself while raising two children as a single parent. While Diane was in college, her husband abandoned the family. Diane and Kendra lived in her car for a brief time, shortly before Courtney was born. After Diane had stabilized her family, they moved into family housing on campus. Although Courtney never met her father, she thrived with her mother's approval while Kendra rebelled.

When Courtney landed her job at MLK, her drug addicted sister said she was wasting her gift of beauty on teaching, that she could make more money working in another occupation, such as media. Courtney ignored her sister's opinion, believing that teaching was her gift, not her beauty.

After reading her emails, Courtney closed her laptop, locked her office door and walked into the cafeteria. "Ready to go Gabriel?"

Gabriel neatly placed his crayons back into the box. "I'm ready Auntie."

Courtney drove Gabriel home like she did every day during the school year and prepared dinner. Her cell phone rang as soon as she opened her front door.

"Hey you."

"What are you doing tonight? It's Friday night. Have dinner with me. I have something to ask you."

"Why don't you come over here? I'm frying fish."

"Emm, that sounds good. What kind."

"Red Snapper."

"I'll be right over."

An hour later, Carter knocked on Courtney's door.

Running to the door, Gabriel let Carter inside.

"What did I tell you about answering the door, Gabriel?" Courtney warned.

"I know Auntie, but I can tell by his footsteps, that it's Uncle Carter."

"You don't know for sure who's at the door. I told you I will answer the door." Courtney opened the door.

"Hi, Uncle Carter."

Carter rubbed the top of Gabriel's head, "Hey there, Buddy. How are you doing?"

Carter took a step closer to Courtney. "How are

you doing beautiful?"

Holding a spatula in her hand and wearing a chef's apron, Courtney kissed Carter with her eyes. Carter pulled her into his embrace, pressing his lips against hers in a kiss. Courtney lowered her arm, dripping olive oil on the hardwood floor from the spatula. "You came right on time."

"Yuk." Gabriel covered his eyes as they kissed.

Carter followed Courtney and Gabriel into the kitchen that smelled of fish and hot water cornbread.

"Gabriel, wash your hands for dinner."

Carter turned his attention away from Courtney and gave Gabriel a gentle look.

Obediently, Gabriel pulled a chair up to the sink and washed his hands.

Courtney turned over the fish in one frying pan and the hot water cornbread in the other.

"I haven't had hot water cornbread in a long time," Carter said thinking about the last time he'd eaten it at a Soul Food restaurant.

Courtney took a pinch-off of a piece she had taken out before he arrived. "Here taste this," she said putting it into his mouth.

The crunchy cornbread flavored with Louisiana

seasoning melted in Carter's mouth. "Emm, this is good," he said. "I'm so glad you know how to cook. I can't wait for dinner."

"So what did you have to ask me?"

"I'll ask you after we eat dinner."

Courtney reheated some leftover collard greens she had frozen from Sunday dinner and finished frying the fish. After Carter had poured three glasses of lemonade, they all enjoyed the meal at the kitchen table filled with Louisiana Hot Sauce and other condiments.

After dinner, Gabriel followed them into the living room.

Courtney bent her head down to Gabriel's level and said, "Gabriel, I want to talk to Uncle Carter alone. Go to your room and do your homework."

"But, I haven't seen Uncle Carter all week."

"I missed you too Buddy." Carter interrupted. "Can you let me talk to your Auntie alone for this one time? It would mean a lot to me."

"Okay. I'll go and do my homework, but only if you promise to look at Ratatouille with me when you finish talking to Auntie Courtney."

"I promise. Scout's honor" Carter said raising up two fingers.

Gabriel went back into his room while Carter and Courtney sat on the black leather sofa centered in front of the fireplace.

Courtney handed Carter a flyer for the Father and Son Day at the Ranch. Carter looked at the flyer and saw that fathers and sons were supposed to dress up in cowboy gear and ride horses at a local ranch.

Courtney looked at Carter with sad eyes. "He wanted to go so badly, but I had to tell him he couldn't go."

Carter turned around to face Courtney on the sofa. "Why did you tell him that?"

"I don't like to make promises I can't keep, and I didn't want to assume you would take him."

"Don't you know me better than that by now?"

Courtney's eyes brightened.

"I told you, Courtney. I love you and Gabriel. You both come as a package. I would love to take Gabriel to Father and Son Day."

Courtney gave Carter a serious look. "Don't promise him you're going to take him if you can't keep it."

Carter looked at the date on the flyer. "I promise, I'll take him. You can let him out of the dungeon now and give him the good news."

"Why don't we go and tell him together." Courtney knocked on Gabriel's door before entering his bedroom. "Gabriel, Uncle Carter has something to tell you."

Gabriel looked at Carter with big round eyes.

"Gabe, how's about you and me moseying along to the Father and Son Day at the Ranch for a horseback ride."

Gabriel jumped up into Carter's arms, "Thank you, Uncle Carter, thank you, thank you, thank you."

Carter started laughing. It was little things like this that made life worth living. "You're welcome, Buddy."

***

For the next few months, Carter came to Courtney's home every day after work to eat dinner. Courtney had never been happier in her life spending evenings, having dinner with Carter.

One evening Carter said, "I want to introduce you and Gabriel to my family for Sunday dinner."

"Only if you promise to attend my Christmas party for the students enrolled in my after school program."

"I'll be there," Carter said.

"I can't wait to meet your family," Courtney said.

***

Carter had gotten the word out to the family that he wanted to introduce them to his fiancée. He had told Kenton all about his desire to marry Courtney and made him promise to keep his mouth shut. Kenton didn't even tell his wife, Briana. Instead, he advised Carter to purchase a ring for Courtney from Tiffany's in Walnut Creek where he'd purchased Briana's ring.

When Carter drove around the circular driveway at the Underwood estate winery, Jimmie the butler stood patiently by the open door, waiting for Carter, Courtney and Gabriel to enter. He led them through the foyer into the spacious living room where the entire family sat on white upholstered sofas and chairs. Henrietta sat in her wheelchair near the entrance to the dining room.

"They're here," Kenton announced to the family.

Carter, Courtney, and Gabriel stepped into the living room. All of the men stood up to greet Courtney.

"Courtney." Ashley held out her arms to welcome Ashley, her sorority sister.

They both flashed sorority signs with their hands and laughed.

"It's good seeing you again, Ashley. I wanted to spend time with you after the wedding, but you and Justin were busy taking photographs. I'd like to spend more time with you now that you're back, but I know you're probably busy with your wifely duties."

"I'm back to work at the spa. I'll call you and catch up with what you and Carter have been doing. We had fun sailing down to South America. We were going to sail to Europe and Asia, but I began to have problems with sea sickness like I told you, and so we cut our honeymoon short."

"Wow. Your honeymoon sounds amazing."

Carter saw Ashley dominating the conversation. He cleared his throat loudly to get everyone's attention. "Family, I'd like you to meet Courtney Oliver and Gabriel Oliver. Courtney is my fiancée."

Chrystal stood up but fell back into her overstuffed chair. She'd never seen Carter with a woman before. Briana looked up from Jonathan sitting in her lap, holding her fingers.

Ashley hugged Courtney. "Congratulations."

"You're going to love the Underwood family."

Kenton, Justin, and Brandon walked up to

Courtney and hugged her.

"Nice pick, Carter," Justin said, winking his eye at Carter.

All three men looked at Gabriel holding Carter's hand. Gabriel politely held out his hand ready for a handshake.

Kenton smiled and shook Gabriel's hand.

"Pleased to meet you, Sir," Gabriel said politely.

Justin raised a curious brow before shaking Gabriel's hand.

"Pleased to meet you, Sir."

Finally, Brandon shook Gabriel's hand.

"Pleased to meet you, Sir."

Carter walked with Courtney and Gabriel over to Henrietta still weak from her heart attack, but she managed to meet them while sitting in her wheelchair.

Gabriel put his left hand in front of his stomach and his right hand behind his back and bowed to Henrietta. "How do you do ma'am."

Happiness shone in Henrietta's cataract eyes as she scanned the polite, well-trained child.

Courtney walked up to Henrietta to shake her

hand.

"We don't shake hands around here honey."

"Granny is still recovering from a heart attack," Carter said to Courtney.

Courtney kissed Henrietta on the cheek. "Nice to meet you Mrs. Underwood."

Henrietta looked Courtney over with approval and said, "I remember you from the hospital. You and Gabriel can call me Granny."

Still holding Carter's hand, Gabriel looked up into Carter's eyes and said, "I like Granny, Uncle Carter."

Standing nearby, Brandon parroted Gabriel. "Uncle Carter?" He gave Carter a probing look.

"I'll explain it at the dinner table," Carter said to Brandon.

Briana had brought dinner over from her restaurant earlier because she couldn't stand Ruby's, cooking. Ruby had been Henrietta's cook for years and cooked bland meals to keep Henrietta's cholesterol down.

Ruby came into the living room and announced, that dinner was ready.

Everyone filed into the formal dining room.

Jimmie pushed Henrietta's wheelchair to the head of the table. She motioned for Carter and Courtney to sit in the empty chairs next to her. Carter decided to sit next to Henrietta so she could not ask Courtney too many personal questions. Courtney sat next to Carter, and across from Ashley.

Kenton tasted and approved a bottle of cabernet for the table while Briana put Jonathan in his high chair.

Determined to find out as much as she could about Courtney, Henrietta asked Courtney about her family.

Courtney answered Henrietta's question as all eyes were on her. "My mother is Dr. Diane Oliver, Professor of Humanities at the University of California.

"What about your father?" Henrietta asked.

Courtney couldn't answer Henrietta's question because she didn't want everyone to know she didn't know her father.

Carter gave his grandmother a hard look and changed the subject. "Brandon, how are the labels coming for the white wines?"

Brandon scrolled through his email messages and didn't hear Carter's question.

Henrietta got the message.

Ashley knew Courtney didn't know her father, so she changed the direction of the conversation. "Justin and I went to Corcovado Mountain in Rio de Janeiro and saw the Christ the Redeemer statue. It was huge, more than two thousand feet high."

"I'd love to see it one day," Courtney said to Ashley.

"So what do you do?" Henrietta asked.

"I'm a teacher."

Henrietta's eyes widened. "A teacher. What grade?"

"Fourth grade."

"I guess teaching runs in your family."

"Yes. It does. Two of my mother's sisters are teachers—one is a music teacher at the University of Illinois, and the other is a teacher at Spellman College in Atlanta."

"I have a question, Carter." Brandon asked. How are you going to run Underwood Technologies in Silicon Valley if you are working at the winery?

"I have to be honest with you Brandon." Carter leaned back in his chair. "I just finished developing some software to run my new artificial liver. I'm not interested in creating any more medical devices.

I've decided to leave Sandeep in charge of running the day to day activities at Underwood Technologies.

"I want to spend my extra time working in the winery and starting a family." Suddenly, Carter's cell phone rang. It was Sandeep. "Speak of the Devil. It's Sandeep from UT. Excuse me, I need to take this call." Carter got up from the table and walked into the living room and spoke to Sandeep.

"Carter. You've got a problem. Reginald wants the Board to vote him in as the new CEO."

Chapter 10

Early Monday morning, Carter took a helicopter ride to his office in Silicon Valley amidst the brisk December wind blowing on his face. Sandeep's urgent call during dinner last night worried Carter all night long. What was Reginald doing? Was he trying to take control of Underwood Technologies? Carter had to find out, so he decided to make a surprise visit today.

As the helicopter hovered over the San Francisco Peninsula, Carter began thinking about his plan to prevent Reginald from taking over the business Carter had built from the ground up. Carter's position as CEO depended on satisfying the Board of Directors led by Reginald Ainsworth, his college roommate from Stanford, University. Carter could have kicked himself for trusting Reginald in that position, especially after he saw how obsessive Reginald had become over accumulating money.

Carter's innovative imagination drove him. Reginald's flat out greed drove him. Carter would have never voted for Reginald as Chairman of the Board if he'd known he would try to take control over Underwood Technologies. All Reginald needed was another three percent of the stock to take the controlling vote in the company.

When Carter arrived at the Underwood

Technologies building, he walked through the front door.

"Good morning Mr. Underwood," the receptionist greeted.

"Good morning Uma. Where's Sandeep?"

"He's in a meeting with the board members," she pointed to the Sierra Conference Room down the hall.

Carter heard Reginald's voice as he walked in.

"Carter's absence is impacting our business."

"What is the problem?" one board member asked.

Reginald fired back angrily. "Carter has taken a leave of absence to work at his family's winery instead of here."

"What has he specifically not done?"

"Since his artificial liver invention, he has not come up with any new medical devices. He's giving our competition a chance to eat up our market share."

"What do you think we should do?"

"I think the Board needs to restructure Underwood Technologies. As a private corporation, our bylaws state that we have the authority to select a new CEO whenever we need a corporate restructure. I think we need to restructure our corporation in order to regain our market share."

That was it! Carter had heard enough. As the CEO of Underwood Technologies, Carter had authority over all of the employees, operatives, officers, and other executives. But his position as CEO, in addition to time spent developing medical devices, had caused him to suffer from burnout. He no longer wanted to be the CEO. He wanted out, but Reginald had another thing coming if he thought he could take over Carter's company and become the new CEO. Carter decided to work on his plan behind the scenes. "So Reginald wants the Board to vote for a new CEO. Okay, but he'll never become the CEO of the company I built from scratch."

Carter went into his office and texted Sandeep, who sat in the Board meeting horrified by the discussion.

Sandeep texted him back. "Reginald is planning a vote for a new CEO at the next Board of Director's meeting. One of the members just nominated Reginald."

Carter texted him back. "Do you want to be the CEO of Underwood Technologies since you've been handling my duties in my absence?"

"Sure. I would love to," Sandeep texted back.

"I'll get you the votes. Some of the board

members owe me some big favors, and I'm going to cash them. I had planned to step down from being CEO anyway. My life is going in a completely new direction, and I have never been happier."

"Good for you, Carter. I'll keep you posted on what's happening in the board meetings."

"Thanks, Deep."

Carter spent the night at his home in Hillsborough. First he called Courtney and told her he was staying at his house, and then he called the board member and made deals with each one who owed him a favor. He asked them to nominate and vote for Sandeep as CEO instead of Reginald, and to nominate and vote for him as the new Chairman of the Board--a position Carter knew he could perform because it required less time and commitment.

***

Carter went back to Napa the next day because he'd promised Courtney he would attend her Christmas Party at Martin Luther King Elementary School.

He stood in front of his mirror buttoning the cuffs on his light blue cotton shirt tucked inside his navy trousers. He wasn't one for what he and his friends called getting suited up. He preferred dressing casual every chance he got. After patting a spicy aftershave on his cheeks, he jumped into his

Tesla and drove to the MLK Christmas party.

Carter pulled up to the cyclone fence surrounding MLK School. He looked around at all of the rundown buildings dominating the neighborhood with gang signs spray painted on every single one. He lowered his head, shaking it, as he turned off his car. He wondered how Courtney's students could survive in such an environment.

***

Christmas music filled the cafeteria, drowned out by children laughing, talking, and horsing around, seated at five rows of long tables pushed together. Off to the side, near Courtney's office, Carter saw a group of mother's arranging punch, cookies and spaghetti in plates and saucers on tables pushed against the wall. A wide grin covered Carter's face when he looked ahead and saw Courtney sitting on the stage next to a decorated live Christmas tree. He saw the brightly wrapped gifts with glittery bows arranged artfully under the tree. Courtney had told him that local employees and churches had donated gifts to the children enrolled in the After School Program. The joy on the children's faces brought a lump to his throat.

Courtney motioned for one of the teenage volunteers to help with the distribution of the gifts. She walked down the side stairs, past the buffet tables and met Carter still standing in the doorway, dazed with the scene before his eyes. He'd never attended a Christmas party filled with so many children.

"Well, I see you made it," Courtney said greeting him with a big smile.

"Told you I wouldn't miss this party for anything." Happy for the experience, Carter looked Courtney over, wearing her Santa hat and red dress. "You look beautiful, Courtney."

"Thank you, Carter. I'm glad you like my snazzy little outfit. Come on. Let's get some punch and I'll introduce you to the volunteers."

They walked over to the buffet table, and Courtney introduced Carter to all of the mothers who were a mixture of diverse races and cultures, some spoke little or no English.

"Ladies, this is Carter Underwood." She didn't mention he was her boyfriend because she knew they would start asking personal questions.

Courtney watched the teenage and young mothers surround Carter and welcome him to the party. All she heard was Carter saying thank you over and over to each woman.

Courtney broke away from the mother's and found two fold up chairs at an empty table in the back. "Let's sit over here."

Courtney saw Gabriel break away from his friends.

"Hi, Uncle Carter."

"Hi, Gabriel. Having fun?"

"Yeah. See you later." He ran back over to his friends sitting at the table.

As soon as Gabriel left, a little boy walked through the door. Courtney got his attention.

"Jamal." She motioned for him to come over. "I have someone for you to meet." She turned to Carter.

"Jamal, this is Mr. Underwood."

Jamal looked at Carter with bright glossy eyes and an ashy face, his smile revealed a chipped tooth. "Hello, Mr. Underwood," Jamal said politely.

"Jamal is one of my brightest students." Courtney smiled at Carter.

"What are some of your favorite subjects Jamal?" Carter asked

"Math and Science."

"You sound like you need to enroll in the STEM program."

"What's that?"

"STEM stands for science, technology, engineering, and mathematics."

"Sounds like fun," Jamal said standing with a wide stance holding his hands behind his back.

Carter looked Jamal over and saw that he wasn't wearing a coat in the freezing weather. He analyzed the boy further and saw duct tape holding his sneakers together. Shocked at the sight of Jamal's shoes, Carter's heart sank to a new low. He had to do something.

Courtney could read Carter's mind. She tried to change the subject. "Jamal is good in math, but he needs to work on his spelling," Courtney said.

Carter still couldn't get his mind off of Jamal's sneakers. He focused on the boy. "Do you like computers?"

"Yes. My favorite game is Call of Duty."

A group of boys called Jamal to come over to join them at their table.

"Go ahead, and join your friends," Courtney said. After Jamal had left, she turned to Carter and smiled.

"I want to help Jamal and any of your other students learn technical skills to help them get out of this neighborhood."

"How do you plan to do that?"

"Maybe have some of the employees from UT

volunteer to teach coding to the students."

"When would your employees do that?"

"I don't know. Perhaps on weekends."

"Jamal and most of my students don't have access to computers at home."

"Then we'll have to give them access to computers here at school."

"But MLK doesn't have a computer lab."

"Then we'll have to make one."

"Look, your idea sounds great, Carter, but we'd have to get approval from the school district to add a computer lab, and computers. Where are these computers going to come from?"

"From Underwood Technologies. We donate computers all the time to schools."

Courtney sat in her chair and stared at Carter. "What a blessing."

"It would be my pleasure to help your students."

Courtney paused for a moment giving Carter an affectionate look. She quickly regained her senses and turned her focus back to the party. "It's time to hand out the Christmas gifts. Do you want to come on stage with me and help hand them out?"

"No. You go ahead. I'll sit right here, drink my punch and observe."

Carter watched Courtney walk back on stage. She sat in her chair and had one of the student volunteers dressed as an elf hand her the presents. She called out the names of the children who ran up on the stage and happily took their presents with big smiles on their faces. Carter had never felt so warm or good in his life.

Near the end of the gift distribution, Carter watched the mother's clean up the mess.

Courtney walked down from the stage. "Well, what do you think about our little Christmas party?"

"This was the best Christmas party I've ever attended."

"I have one question for you, Courtney?"

"What's that?"

"Did you see Jamal's shoes being held together with duct tape?"

"Yes. I did."

"Why didn't you buy him a new pair of shoes?"

"I did. I bought him a pair of Air Jordan sneakers, but the neighborhood teenagers beat him up and stole them. That's one of the downfalls of living in this neighborhood. Many of my students live in homeless shelters and transition housing. The lucky ones live in the projects."

"I want to donate a Christmas present to each of your students. I'm going to open an account at the GAP. I want you to purchase shoes and clothing for all of them."

"What?" Courtney stared at Carter in disbelief. She shook her head to break out of the shock of his statement. "That shouldn't be a problem. I have all of their clothing and shoe sizes. I know their mothers will be happy.

"Make sure you get them all winter coats too. Underwood Technologies makes donations to organizations every single day. I want to include the students in your after school program."

"Do you want to come with me to purchase the clothing?" Courtney asked.

"Why don't you make it easy on yourself and order the clothing online."

"What a good idea."

Carter watched the mothers pack away the last of the food before walking home with their children.

"Come on. Let's get Gabriel and go home," Carter said.

"Okay."

When they reached Courtney's car, Carter opened her car door. Before she and Gabriel entered, Carter kissed her. "I'll see you at your house."

Feeling an eager affection coming from Carter, Courtney leaned into him kissing him softly. Carter returned with a slow drugging kiss.

Courtney stepped into her car and said, "Carter, I think you are an honorable, good man. I am the luckiest woman in the world."

Carter closed her door and made sure she and Gabriel were safely buckled up in their seatbelts before he left. On the way to his car, Carter passed a for sale sign posted in front of a large apartment building next to the school. He thought about purchasing the property and using it to house some of the homeless students.

***

Later that night as Carter lay in bed holding Courtney in his arms, he thought of the duct tape holding Jamal's shoes together. Something about the Christmas party had changed Carter's heart and mind forever. He had to help the students. If he didn't help, then who would? He wanted his corporation to do more to help the underperforming schools. He couldn't turn a blind eye to what he saw.

Chapter 11

The next morning, Carter took his helicopter to his office. He wanted to attend the Board of Directors meeting today and request a vote to donate computers to the MLK After School Program. Underwood Technologies voted on hefty financial donations to non-profit organizations every meeting. He wanted to add MLK to the donor list. He didn't expect much support from Reginald, but he knew he could depend on Sandeep and a few other board members.

When he arrived at his office, he called ahead to key members and asked for them to vote for Sandeep for CEO, himself for Chairman of the Board, and to approve the computer donation. Most of the board members complied with his request because they didn't want to go along with Reginald's plan to take over the company.

At the meeting, the board members sat around the large conference table with Reginald sitting at the head. Reginald opened the meeting.

"At our last meeting we discussed voting for a new CEO and Chairman of the Board to restructure the company. We can earn billions if we can regain our market share. Besides Underwood Technologies has promised to provide a new line of medical devices to some high profile clients. But now we will not be able to live up to our obligations. The Board needs to retire Carter as CEO since he's decided to take a leave of absence."

The board members began talking in low voices.

"Are there any nominations on the table for a new CEO?" Reginald asked.

"I nominate Sandeep Gupta," Carter said walking into the board room. After listening to Reginald's little speech, Carter saw himself in Reginald. But, he no longer wanted to make money his God—that kind of thinking was over.

All heads turned around as Carter entered the board room.

Startled at Carter's nomination, Reginald took a step backward and asked, "Are there any other nominations?"

One board member said, "I nominate Reginald Ainsworth for CEO."

Reginald smiled. "Are there any more nominations?"

Voices lowered, and the room became completely quiet.

"Are there any nominations for the office of Chairman of the Board of Directors?"

Sandeep said, "I nominate Carter Underwood."

Fire glazed in Reginald's eyes as if his worst enemy stabbed him in the back. He paused to regain his composure. "Are there any more nominations for the office of Chairman of the Board of Directors?" Reginald looked around the room at the board members who avoided eye contact. The room became quiet once again.

"Now we'll have the vote."

The secretary passed around a slate of candidates to all of the board members except Reginald. As the Chairman of the Board, he could only vote to break a tie. When the slates came back in, the election committee counted the votes and found Sandeep had won the most votes as CEO and Carter had won as Chairman of the Board.

Reginald's face turned beet red. "Is there any new business?"

Carter stood up. "I'd like to motion for the board to add the MLK after school program to our donation list to purchase new computers."

"I second that motion," Sandeep said.

Everyone voted overwhelmingly for Carter's motion, except Reginald, who sat brooding in his seat. Reginald stood up. "I don't think Underwood Technologies should waste money donating computers to those inner city kids. We need supply more medical devices to bring in more income." Reginald said defiantly.

The board approved the donation to MLK without Reginald's support.

Now that he held no office, Reginald sat in his chair seething.

***

That night Carter returned to Courtney's house.

"How did your Board meeting go today?"

"I was elected Chairman of the Board."

"I thought you were CEO."

"We elected Sandeep as the new CEO."

"What about you, how did your day go at school?"

"If I didn't know any better, I would think the entire school has recently enrolled in the after-school program."

"What happened?"

"Since my students passed the national test with flying colors, more students are enrolling in my after school program every day. The cafeteria is almost full."

Carter smiled. "I'm happy to hear you have more children enrolled in the program. As far as I'm concerned, the more the better." He wrapped his arm around her shoulder. "Did you get a chance to order clothing for the students?"

"I started working on my list last week."

Carter smiled. "Good. Don't forget to purchase winter coats for them."

"I won't."

Carter had lived a privileged life and had no idea how it felt to go to school in the winter months, hungry and cold without a coat, or to learn without proper tools to get a good education. After the Christmas party, Carter was no longer interested in living an extravagant lifestyle. He'd come to the conclusion, he didn't need to travel the world to get a new perspective on life. He'd found his new perspective in the faces of Courtney, Gabriel and his family. He wanted to use his money to help children like Jamal. He'd become fed up with watching struggling schools on the news trying to survive in today's economy. Carter loved how he felt when he helped change someone's life, especially Courtney's students who he believed did not have enough money to learn.

"The Board voted to donate computers to MLK." Carter said while stroking Courtney's shoulders with the tips of his fingers.

"But where are we going to put them? We don't have any space."

"Maybe I can donate a portable building and turn it into a computer lab."

"A computer lab." Courtney's eyes sparkled. "That would be a blessing, Carter."

"When can we get the building?"

"I'll begin working on this project after I test the software to run the winery's bottling operation." Carter said.

"Carter, are you sure you're not biting off more than you can chew with the computers?"

"I'm not going to change my mind. I'm as good as my word no matter what happens."

***

The next morning, Carter and Kenton stood in the bottling warehouse watching Carter start the software from the computer room. Carter pressed the enter button to run the test. He walked through the door listening as the loud machinery calibrated to bottle Kenton's first production of white wines.

Kenton made sure the bottles had been sterilized and sanitized. He double-checked the wine was sixty degrees or warmer because the glue from the labels would not adhere if the bottles were cold or wet from condensation.

Kenton watched white wine bottles grouped six

to a row roll down a long line on the stainless steel conveyor belt. "Today, we're bottling Riesling for my 2015 vintage." Kenton said proudly.

Carter watched to ensure the automated process propelled the empty bottles along the conveyor belt smoothly, filling, corking and sealing the wine. If everything ran correctly, workers would place labels on the wine and pack the wine in cases at the end of the conveyor belt. Carter stuck out his chest as he saw there were no glitches in the bottling process.

"Kenton yelled to Carter over the loud machinery. "We'll double our profits, now that we're growing white grapes, our winery will produce over two million bottles per year."

Kenton came over and hugged Carter when he saw there were no bottlenecks in the bottling operation. "Job well-done, Brother."

Carter couldn't remember the last time he'd felt prouder of helping his family. "You're welcome, Bro."

***

Two weeks later Carter stood behind the cafeteria at MLK, directing a big rig driver carrying the portable building on a flatbed. Carter held out his right hand directing the driver to turn more to the right. Then he held out his left hand directing him to turn more to the left. After the driver had positioned the portable building behind the cafeteria in the exact spot where it would stand, Carter held out both hand for the driver to stop.

Courtney watched through the cafeteria's back window. "It's a huge double sized building," Courtney said to another teacher.

"I am excited to see some positive changes going on at our school," the teacher replied.

Courtney watched the driver lower the building onto the asphalt ground. "We're supposed to get the computers installed after the building is set up."

"Do we have a computer science teacher?"

"Yes. Our science teacher, Mr. Perry will teach computer classes."

Courtney walked through the back door of the cafeteria to talk to Carter. "So what's next, Carter?"

"The contractors are going to hook up electricity and then hardwire the building."

"What about security?"

"A security company is scheduled to come out tomorrow to install a system for the building."

The next day Courtney watched as Carter and the computer vendor installed the computers and servers. Then she watched as the security company installed a security system. The security tech trained

Courtney, the principal, and teachers how to use the security alarm.

***

Later that night, Courtney said to Carter. "Donating the computer lab to the school is a wonderful thing for the students. I haven't seen your bad side with my students. All I see is a kind man who has been nothing but a blessing."

Carter laughed. "Ha. I beg to differ with you. I have a dark side. I'm far from perfect."

"Okay, Darth Vader. Tell me about your dark side."

"I'll let you find out on your own. Right now I want to make sweet love to you," he said, easing her onto the bed.

"Hold on Cowboy. You know we need to wait until Gabriel goes to sleep."

"Okay, okay. But we always lock your bedroom door after he goes to sleep."

"I've always taught him to knock before entering my bedroom in case I'm dressing or if he wakes up and finds you sleeping in my bed."

"I know, but I don't like locking the door," Courtney said.

"Yeah, yeah, yeah. Come here woman."

They made love all night long. Both were late to work late the next morning.

***

At eleven o'clock in the morning, Reginald Ainsworth picked up his tenth shot of Jack Daniel's in an upscale Silicon Valley bar and drank deeply. His disheveled hair and unshaven face announced he was a loser to the world. His plot to become CEO of Underwood Technologies had backfired, and he no longer held the office of Chairman of the Board of Directors.

He and Sandeep joined Carter's newly formed company, Underwood Technologies before they all graduated from college. Carter was supposed to build the medical devices and code the software to run the instruments he built, Sandeep was to provide his expert medical advice to Carter and Reginald was to provide marketing services for the business. They all split a percentage of the shares three ways with Carter holding the majority of shares. Now Reginald held no office and had no power. Seething with white hot anger, Reginald thought of ways to get back at Carter.

Chapter 12

Later that night Courtney couldn't sleep. She went into the kitchen and fixed a cup of warm cocoa. She picked up the phone and called her mother, who stayed up all hours of the night.

"Mama?"

"Courtney. How are you doing baby?" She said with a cheerful voice.

"You busy?"

"No. Sitting here putting a puzzle together."

"I have some good news, Mama."

"You know I'm always ready to hear some good news."

"Remember Carter Underwood, the guy I met at Ashley's wedding."

"Yes, I remember hearing you talk about him. Gabriel kind of gravitated to him?"

"He gave me a ring. I think he wants to marry me."

Silence.

172

"Mama? Are you there?"

"Yes, I'm here baby."

"Well, what do you think?"

"It's not a matter of what I think. It's a matter of what you think. You'll have to live with the man—not me. He sounds like a good man from what you tell me. He treats you and Gabriel well, comes from a good family and owns his own business. What more can you ask for in a man. When are you all getting married?"

"I don't know? We've only known each other for six months."

"Well, give it some time baby. A man always puts on his best face in the beginning, trust me—I know."

"You're talking about Daddy?" Courtney said, stirring her hot cocoa. Her thoughts drifted to her father who had abandoned her when she was a baby. When she was old enough to understand her father didn't want her, Courtney felt deeply rejected, and never expressed to her mother how she subconsciously expected to be abandoned in her romantic relationships. Maybe her mother knew how she felt, and that's why she tried to control Courtney and her sister so much. Courtney stared into space, taking a sip of her cocoa.

"Yes, honey. But all men are not like your

father."

"I believe you Mama, but what if Carter breaks my heart and leaves me hanging like Daddy?"

"Don't compare Carter to your father. Your father was a pretty boy who thought he was God's gift to women. He couldn't keep his hands off of other women, and then he left me with you and your sister to raise while putting myself through college." She picked up a puzzle piece staring at it for a moment while thinking about her feelings toward her ex-husband. "He put on his best face before I married him."

Courtney had heard the story a million times before. "Carter told me he has never loved a woman before."

"At least you know he's not a womanizer," she said before sliding the puzzle piece in its correct location.

"No. Carter's more like a handsome nerd."

"Nerds are underrated. All I can say to you is give your relationship some time so you can see all sides of Carter—the good, the bad and the ugly. Then make your decision."

"Okay Mama," Courtney said before downing the last drops of her cocoa. "I'll talk to you later. I'm going back to bed."

"Okay, Baby. I love you."

"Love you too Mama." Courtney turned off the kitchen light and climbed back into bed where Carter was snoring. Within minutes, she was out like a light.

***

The next day Carter made a surprise visit to his office in Silicon Valley and told Reginald to meet him in the large conference room. He had a bone to pick with him for his betrayal. Reginald was in the conference room when Carter arrived. Carter walked in and closed the door behind him. He walked over to face Reginald, who stood at the head of the conference table. Carter stared at him with a lethal calmness in his eyes. Reginald returned Carter's glare with flat, hard, arrogant eyes.

Carter was more hurt than angry. Since they were roommates at Stanford, Carter had kept his feelings about Reginald's jealousy inside. But now, he had to confront this backstabbing begrudging man, who'd wanted to undermine Underwood Technologies from the beginning. Reginald came from old money in England. His superior attitude couldn't accept the fact Carter was gifted enough to invent medical devices that made them both billionaires. Carter was hurt because he had trusted Reginald and Sandeep like the brothers he believed he never had. Reginald's betrayal had hurt Carter so deeply, that Carter could choke him with his bare hands, but he decided to make sure Reginald would think twice before doing something like this ever again.

"What's wrong Carter? You look angry." Reginald asked as he moved away from the conference table.

"I'm not playing games with you, Reginald." Carter said. His eyes were icy cold. "You ask what's wrong with me. I'll tell you. I trusted you like a brother enough to let you work for my business when we were students. But I don't trust you now as far as I can see. How could you do this to me, Reginald? You're nothing but a backstabbing, traitor." Carter balled up his fists as he walked closer to face Reginald eye to eye. Through gritted teeth Carter barked, "You're fired, Reginald, pack your things and get out of here."

"What do you mean? You can't fire me."

"Why not because you're Chairman of the Board? You forget Reginald, you no longer hold that office. Get out!" Carter took a step closer to Reginald. "I'm telling you this one time. If you ever come near Underwood Technologies employees or the Board of Directors again, you're going to be faced with a restraining order and the Police."

Reginald edged closer to the door all under Carter's icy stare and threat.

After Reginald left, Carter walked out of the conference room as if nothing had happened.

Late in the evening, Carter sat in Courtney's home office typing with ferocious keystrokes on his laptop like there was no tomorrow. When Carter worked, he concentrated on the task at hand, barely noticing anything around him.

Courtney stuck her head in the door. "Carter."

"No answer."

"Carter," she said louder.

"What," Carter barked. You know I hate interruptions when I'm working.

"I don't appreciate your tone of voice," She said feeling hurt.

"I'm sorry, Courtney, but you shouldn't have interrupted me while I'm in the zone."

"But, I need to talk to you, Carter."

Carter turned around from his laptop. He huffed. "What do you need to talk about?"

"The Father and Son Day at the Ranch event is coming up."

"Courtney, can we talk about that at a later time." Carter snapped. "I need to focus on this document. I don't need any distractions right now."

Courtney knew how Carter felt about Reginald trying to vote him out of office. After hearing the seriousness in Carter's voice, she decided to wait. "Sure. We can talk about it later," Courtney said. She wondered how she could reach out to Carter, to help him through the pain of Reginald's betrayal. She said what was in her heart. "I'm in your corner Carter. No matter what, you can talk to me because I love you, and I've got your back."

Carter ignored her words and continued typing his document.

Saddened by his lack of regard to her words, Courtney left and went back into the bedroom.

Minutes later Carter came out of the office and stood in the doorway of the bedroom, looking at Courtney staring at the floor.

"He hurt me. I loved Reginald like a brother, and he sold me out like I was nothing." His voice began to crack.

Courtney walked over to Carter and held him in her arms, rubbing his back.

Chapter 13

Several days later, Courtney interrupted Carter while he was in the office working on his laptop.

"Carter."

"Yeah."

"I'd like to continue our conversation we were supposed to have about Father and Son day at the Ranch."

Carter turned around from his laptop. "When is it?" He asked in an irritated voice. The stress from Reginald's betrayal and problems with the Board of Directors had caused him to fall back into his old hard driving, controlling ways. He knew he was falling back into his old ways and didn't like the way it made him feel. He didn't know of any other way to interact with his Board, other than using his hard-nosed tactics. Otherwise, they'd run all over him and the company.

"The event is next Friday."

"Next Friday I have an important Board meeting to vote to restructure the company. I have to cancel."

"No. You cannot!"

"I'm sorry, but I can't miss this meeting."

"You promised Gabriel you'd take him. I told you not to promise to take him if you couldn't keep your promise."

"I'll make it up to Gabriel."

"Then you'll have to tell him he can't go."

"Where is he now?"

"He's in his room doing his homework."

Carter got up from his computer and walked into Gabriel's room.

"Gabe."

"Yes, Uncle Carter."

"I have something to tell you."

Gabriel looked at Carter with big round eyes.

"Gabe, I can't take you to Father and Son day at the Ranch."

Big tears welled up in Gabriel's eyes. He ran to his bed and started crying. Courtney walked in and held Gabriel while she stared angrily at Carter.

Carter sat next to Courtney, "I'll make it up to you buddy. What if I take you and some of your friends to Disneyland on my private jet? Do you think you'd like that?"

Gabriel stopped crying and listened to Carter's proposition. "Disneyland on your jet?"

"I promise to take you and your friends, all expenses paid the next day after the Father and Son day at the Ranch."

Gabriel sniffled, "Okay."

Courtney gave Carter a hard look. "Gabriel, me and your Uncle need to talk. We'll talk about this later." She got up from the bed and pulled Carter with her.

One thing Courtney couldn't stand was for someone to break promises. She never promised anything to Gabriel for that reason. When she was growing up, her mother disappointed her by breaking her promises on a regular basis. Courtney vowed when she grew up--she would never do that to anyone.

"If you break your promise again, it's over. I have no intention of sharing my life with you if you disappoint Gabriel again."

"You mean, you would break up with me over disappointing Gabriel?"

"Yes. I would."

"Sounds like you want me to be perfect."

"I can deal with most of your imperfections Carter, but not disappointing Gabriel."

"There you go smothering him again."

"I'm not smothering him. He's my nephew, and I'm protecting him from a life of disappointment."

"Disappointment!" Carter yelled. "When have I ever disappointed you before, Courtney?" Carter raised his voice higher. "You make it sound like I disappoint Gabriel all of the time. This is the first time I need to break a promise to him."

"Don't raise your voice at me," Courtney glared through angry eyes.

Gabriel knocked on Courtney's office door. "Why are you guys yelling at each other?"

Carter stared at Courtney while heaving. He had surprised himself with his emotion outburst. Normally, he didn't talk that way to women, but then no woman ever made him feel the way Courtney made him feel.

"I think you should chill out and leave for a while."

"Leave?" Carter turned around with an angry look on his face. "Fine. I'll leave." He closed his laptop, pulled his jacket out of the closet and left. All while Gabriel stood in the doorway crying watching his Uncle leave. After Carter closed the front door, he could hear Gabriel crying loudly like a baby. It broke Carter's heart to cause so much pain to Courtney and Gabriel, but Courtney was right. He needed to take a break and think things through.

Courtney lay in her bed in the darkness of midnight thinking long and hard about whether Carter was family man material or the right man for her. She saw how problems in his company brought out the worse in him. She wondered if she would be able to put up with his dark side if she married him. She pulled the covers over her head and went back to sleep.

***

Carter looked at the clock on his dashboard on his way to his grandmother's house. It was ten o'clock. He opened the door with the key he'd had since he was a teenager and went straight to his room.

"Who does she think she is, throwing me out like that?" Carter asked himself as he undressed for bed. He was mad at himself for yelling at Courtney, but there was nothing he could do about breaking his promise to Gabriel. He felt like the world was closing in on him. First Reginald betrayed him, now Courtney threw him out for breaking a promise.

Carter thought about it. Maybe he took his frustration out on Courtney because he focused on Reginald's shenanigans. Look where that landed him—alone with no fiancée. He had to take control of his behavior that was destroying his life. Before he'd met Courtney, he'd never experienced a lover's quarrel. But now he'd hurt the woman he loved more than himself and felt like he was destroying his life. He sat on the side of the bed looking through his window wondering how he could get Courtney back. He pulled out his cellphone and called her. His call went straight to her voicemail. Humph, she's not taking my calls. He pulled the covers over his head and went to sleep.

The next morning, Carter went to the winery. He stuck his head into Kenton's office. "Hey. You're here."

"Where did you expect me to be?"

"Maybe, out in the vineyards."

"I'm in here looking at Brandon's label designs. Take a look."

Carter walked over and saw the new design had a slight Afrocentric look.

"What do you think? I like the African mask, but do you think it represents our brand?"

"I don't know?" Carter said walking over to the window looking out into the vineyards.

"Okay Carter, I can tell when something is

bothering you. What's wrong?"

"Courtney and I had a fight. She kicked me out of her house."

"You weren't living there. Were you?"

"No. I just spent a lot of time over there."

"What happened?"

"We had an argument over me breaking a promise to Gabriel."

"What promise?"

"I promised to take him to the Father and Son day at the Ranch, but it's on the same day as the Board meeting to vote on the restructuring plan."

"I understand, but kids don't understand broken promises?"

"Yeah. I know. I told Gabriel I would make it up to him."

"How were you going to make it up?"

"By taking him and his friends to Disneyland on my jet the day after the Father and Son day. Gabriel seemed to be okay with it, but then Courtney made a big deal of me breaking my promise and then everything went downhill after that."

Kenton listened. "You both will work it out."

"Maybe so, but I'm also having problems with my business."

"What happened to your business?"

"Reginald Ainsworth, the Chairman of the Board, tried to get the Board to vote him in as the new CEO."

"No."

"Yes."

"Boy, you're getting hit from all directions."

"Tell me about it. Reginald tried to restructure the company."

"Restructure the company?"

"What's wrong with the structure of your company?"

"Nothing. It was a smokescreen, for Reginald to take over as CEO."

"But I thought you didn't want to be the CEO anymore?"

"I don't. But I don't want Reginald, of all people, to hold that office."

"Brother, I didn't know you were going through all of this."

"Yes. And I think I took my frustrations out on Courtney, and now, I've screwed that relationship up."

"Relationships are tough, Brother. My advice to you is to listen to your heart. If you love Courtney, then you need to learn how to compromise because true love is rare, and may not cross your path again. Don't let your ego ruin your life."

"Ego. I don't have an ego?"

"Yes, you do. You are the most self-centered, controlling person I know, Brother."

"Well, maybe I am."

"Carter. You told me you wanted to travel the world and get a new perspective on life. Why would you tell me you wanted to leave your company if it's still rooted in your heart? You simply need to make a choice."

"My heart will always be rooted in the business I created from the ground up. But, I'm no spineless coward either, Bro. I couldn't stand by and let Reginald take over my business like a bully."

"Let me get this right. You told me you were no longer interested in running your business because it sucks up all of your time."

"Yes. My responsibilities are ruining my quality of life. I can't even remember the last time I've been home."

"Have you thought about hiring new employees to help with your workload?

"Yes, but I'm beginning to wonder like there was only one Steve Jobs, there's only one Carter Underwood. No one else can produce superior medical devices like me."

Kenton rolled his eyes. "There goes your ego. Okay. I get it. In my opinion, you need to find someone else to run your company."

"I have. My friend Sandeep. You remember him."

"Yes. He was your college roommate. Good. Then you're halfway there. Let Sandeep run your business. You can always get another business, but you can't always get another mind. Besides the family needs you here at the winery. There is no way you will suffer burnout here."

Carter pulled out his cell phone and called Courtney for the tenth time. She still wasn't taking his calls.

***

Courtney called her mother on her way to work and told her everything. Her mother didn't get involved with Courtney's conversation. She listened to Courtney vent.

"Carter can be very inflexible. He wouldn't cancel his Board meeting so he could take Gabriel to the Father and Son day at school like he promised. That kind of attitude can't be good for a marriage."

"Well, you're inflexible too."

"I am not," Courtney said into her speaker phone."

"Courtney, if you want a successful marriage, you're going to have to learn how to compromise."

"I know how to compromise. "I want a real family Mama." She felt guilty after she'd said she wanted a real family. "I'm sorry Mama. I didn't mean it that way." What she meant was she wanted a husband to go along with her children, but she couldn't say that to her mother.

"Now that he's gone, what are you going to do?"

"I'm going to continue doing what I was doing before I met him. I'm going to teach my fourth graders and take care of Gabriel."

"Speaking of Gabriel, how is he taking the breakup?"

"He cried himself to sleep after our argument. He's been asking about Carter since he left. He misses Carter, and so do I."

"Like I said, you both need to work things out and compromise."

"I hear you, Mama."

***

The day of the board meeting to vote on the restructuring plan had finally come. Carter had spent the night at his home in Hillsborough. He walked slowly around the large conference room table and then stopped abruptly.

"Loyalty," he paused, is a very valuable attribute." He continued walking, around the table looking each member in the eye remembering when they first became members of the board of directors.

"Reginald promised each of you God knows what to vote for his restructuring plan. Reginald Ainsworth no longer works here. Our company doesn't need restructuring. The HR department is hiring expert biomedical engineers from around the globe to continue producing high-quality medical devices. So, make your vote count to strengthen Underwood Technologies.

The board members whispered into each other's ears.

"I'd like to hear a yea or nay from each board member by raising your hands."

Each board member raised his hand to reject

Reginald's restructuring plan.

A wide smile crossed Carter's face as he looked at his Board of Directors full of raised hands in a unanimous vote. He felt like a ton of bricks had been lifted off of his shoulders. "Thank you. I move to adjourn the meeting."

"I second," a member said.

"All in favor say aye."

"Aye."

"All opposed say nay."

Silence.

"Meeting adjourned," Carter said before walking out of the board room.

Carter called Courtney again and left a frustrated message after his call went into her voicemail.

Chapter 14

In the middle of the night, Carter raised his hand to his rapidly beating heart. He thought he had a heart attack. The last face he'd seen before falling asleep was Courtney's. It had been two weeks since he'd last seen her. What was happening to him? He couldn't eat, or sleep, or concentrate. Courtney's face lingered in his mind day and night. He began to take in deep breaths to slow down his heart palpitations.

With a heavy sigh, he lay back down beating his fist on his pillow, realizing he didn't have a heart attack. His heart needed a tune-up that only Courtney could fix. He missed her soft, gentle touch and kisses. He thought about how much fun they had when they went to Lake Anza and Hawaii. He remembered how sexy she looked in her Hawaiian dress and a flower in her hair. He saw her image in mirrors, windows, everywhere he looked.

More than anything, Carter wanted to get back with Courtney and go back to the way they were before he left. But he couldn't because he had burned his bridges with his controlling attitude. Kenton had made Carter understand the importance of compromise in loving relationships. Carter realized he needed to be more flexible and less controlling. He could have kicked himself for being so self-centered, exactly what he was trying to change about himself. But he'd gotten so carried away with the stress with his company, he'd let the woman of his dreams go. He'd come to realize he loved Courtney enough to have a million children with her as long as they could be together.

He'd lost count of the times he'd called her since he had left. She wouldn't return his calls. He could have kicked himself for being so cruel and unfeeling to her in one of his messages. He had to get her back or die trying. Maybe he would go over to her house one day and wait for her to let him inside. In the meantime, he decided to work off his frustration in the winery.

***

Courtney sat on Gabriel's bed with him reading "Toy Story." Gabriel turned over and started whimpering.

"What's wrong Gabe?"

"I miss Uncle Carter. He read that story to me real good."

Courtney lowered the book. "I miss him too."

"Why can't he come back?"

"We had a disagreement, and it's over."

"Why don't you find something you both can agree on? Can't you talk it over like you do with me when we don't agree?"

Stunned by Gabriel's statement, Courtney mulled over his words and exhaled to release her angst. Is it that simple? Just talk it over with Carter? She laughed, feeling lighter in her heart. "Come here Gabriel," She pulled him into her arm and gave him a big hug. "You are a very wise young man!"

***

Saturday afternoon, Courtney decided to take Gabriel over to see her mother and prepare a dinner for her. They arrived at her mother's two-story three bedroom house in the Oakland Hills around noon. Gabriel was the first one to run into the family room and give his grandmother a great big hug. "Hi G. Mama."

"Hi Lil Man," Diane Oliver said greeting her grandson. She told Gabriel to call her G. Mama instead of Grandma because she felt too young for him to call her Grandma, even though she wore floral house dresses and house slippers every day.

Diane leaned back in her black leather recliner, part of her family room furniture, watching a black and white western movie on he big screen TV when Courtney walked in carrying a bag of groceries, placing them on the white tile kitchen island next to the family room.

Courtney walked over to her mother, leaned down and gave her a kiss. "Hi, Mama."

"Hi, Courtney. What are you going to cook?"

"How about a big pot of chicken noodle soup since it's so cold outside."

"That sounds wonderful, Baby."

Courtney went to the kitchen and unpacked the groceries. She washed her hands before placing cut up chicken breasts into a large pot filled with water. While the chicken was cooking, she pulled out a bag of egg noodles, some celery, and other vegetables, slicing them into small pieces.

Gabriel sat in front of the television and turned to his grandmother. "G. Mama," can I turn the TV to the Disney channel?"

"Sure you can, son."

"Suddenly the doorbell rang. Gabriel started to answer the door, but instead looked at Courtney.

"I'll get the door."

Courtney walked to the front door and opened it to, Kendra. Courtney's mouth fell open at the sight of her obviously inebriated sister wearing tight blue jeans and a white loose fitting polyester top with lipstick smudged on the cowl neckline. "Hi, Kendra." She opened the door for her to come inside. Courtney saw a man wearing a bandana tied around his head sitting in an old Chevy Crown Victoria painted a faded gold or light brown parked across the street. "Come inside Kendra."

Courtney's worst nightmare was coming true as she watched her sister waddle down the hall into the family room. Courtney could count the times on one hand Kendra had seen Gabriel since he was born. She walked up to Gabriel sitting in front of the television watching Teenage Mutant Ninja Turtles and hugged him from behind smelling like alcohol. "Hi Gabriel."

"Hi mom." Gabriel turn around and gave his mother a hug and then continued watching his show.

Kendra walked over to her mother who gave her a mean look and hugged her. "Hi, Mama."

"Hello, Kendra," Diane said in a disappointed tone. "What brings you here?"

"I came over her to ask you if I could get Gabriel back."

"Why? So you can get welfare payments?"

"No."

Courtney gave Gabriel a serious look. "Go upstairs and look at TV Gabriel."

"I want him back because he's mine, not Courtney's."

"You're drunk," Diane said.

"No, I'm not. I'll tell you why I want him back. It's because I hate you! You both are turning him against me. He barely spoke to me when I walked in," she said almost stumbling over a throw rug.

Courtney jumped into the conversation. "Okay Kendra, lower your voice and show some respect for Mama or leave."

"Who do you think you are, Courtney to take my baby like you did? Mama always treated you better than me."

Courtney watched her mother's eyes well up with tears. "What's wrong with you Kendra? Stop making, Mama Cry! She's my mother too."

Scared and confused, Gabriel heard the ruckus and came back downstairs.

"Gabriel, who do you want to stay with, me or Courtney?"

"I want to be with you, Mother, but I want to live with Aunt Courtney too."

"See there. You both turned him against me."

"Kendra, no court is going to allow you to take Gabriel back until you go into a drug rehabilitation program."

"I've already done that. I've been clean for a month."

Courtney looked into Kendra's glassy eyes. "You're lying."

"I would rather Gabriel stay in a foster home before I would let him continue to stay with you so you could poison his mind against me."

"You're doing a pretty good job of doing that yourself coming over here drunk and high on who knows what."

Kendra staggered again. "I'm going to get my man."

"Kendra, do you want that for Gabriel?"

"I don't care. He's my baby." Kendra walked to the door and waved to her boyfriend.

Courtney watched in horror as Kendra's boyfriend came inside, yelling and barking at Courtney and her mother about how they took Gabriel from his biological mother.

Courtney held Gabriel in her arms as he began to cry. "I'm not going to let you ruin Gabriel," she said to her sister.

"I know you're not." She turned to her boyfriend and said. "Go to the car, Baby." After her boyfriend had left, Kendra snatched Gabriel from Courtney's arms and ran out the door.

Courtney ran out the house, following Kendra

and her boyfriend before they could get away.

Gabriel jumped out of the car and ran into Courtney's arms. Courtney and Gabriel locked themselves inside her car and drove back home.

"It's not over," Kendra yelled out.

For the next few days, Gabriel was afraid to sleep in his room by himself. He needed to be under Courtney all of the time, so Courtney let him sleep in her room at night to feel safe.

One night, Courtney lay in bed thinking about how she could protect Gabriel from Kendra kidnapping him. She decided to seek out a lawyer to place a restraining order on her sister.

Chapter 15

Carter lifted a heavy case of wine and placed it on a palette as Kenton walked into the warehouse from the cellar.

Kenton walked over to Carter. "Working like a maniac is not going to bring her back. We pay laborers very well to do this work."

"I know. I'm trying to work off my frustration. She won't return my calls."

"You need to do what I did to get Briana back after she left me."

"What did you do?"

"I did what Grandfather did to get Granny back."

"What's that?"

"Grandfather Frank went over to Granny's house, took her by the hand and told her daddy he was taking his wife back home."

"What did Granny do?"

"She went with him and never left him again."

"My situation is different."

"Maybe so, but you're not going to get Courtney back by stocking cases of wine on this palette."

Carter dropped the last case. "I'm going to go over there later today and sit outside until she lets me in."

"There you go, Brother. Go over there and talk to her."

Carter took off his suede work gloves and threw them on the palette. "Thanks, Bro. I needed your boost."

***

Carter went into his room and took a shower thinking about what he was going to say to Courtney. He would say and do anything to get her back. After showering and shaving, he patted a woodsy aftershave on his face and dressed in a pair of khaki trousers and a light blue shirt.

He drove over to her house and waited until he saw her pull up in her driveway with Gabriel.

Gabriel was the first one to notice Carter's car parked on the street. "Uncle Carter, Uncle Carter!" Gabriel ran up to Carter, who got out of his car and hugged Carter tightly. "I missed you, Uncle Carter."

"I missed you too, Buddy. Why don't you go into the house while I talk to your Aunt?"

"Okay. Gabriel skipped to the car, removed his backpack larger than him while thinking about all of the banned sugary snacks he could find.

Courtney opened her car door and watched Carter standing by the curbside. "Come inside," she said. She opened the front door while Gabriel ran past her as she stood on the threshold waiting for Carter.

Carter walked inside deliberately brushing her on the way.

Courtney got a whiff of his sexy aftershave cologne when he passed her.

"I came to talk to you, Courtney." He chose his words carefully so he wouldn't hurt her feelings. "I'm sorry, Courtney. Please forgive me for yelling at you and breaking my promise to Gabriel."

"I forgive you for raising your voice, but I need to explain why I have a problem with people making promises they can't keep. Before I do that," she paused. "A lot has happened since I last saw you."

Carter gave her an anxious look. "What happened?"

"Kendra tried to kidnap Gabriel."

"What!"

"She tried to snatch him while we were at my mother house."

"What did you do?"

"I took him back."

"I mean, how are you going to handle this legally?"

"I'm going to call a lawyer to place a restraining order on her."

"I have a lawyer for you—Justin. He'll get a restraining order."

Carter took Courtney by the hand and walked with her to the sofa. "That must have scared you to death.""

"It did. Gabriel recently went back to sleeping in his room. He slept in my bed days after that incident."

"Well, don't worry. I'll call Justin tonight, and he can get the paperwork started tomorrow. So to get back to why we broke up, tell me why you have a problem with people making promises they can't keep."

"When I was growing up, my mother broke promises to me all of the time. It got to the point when I stopped believing her. I didn't want that to happen to us."

"Oh baby, I'm sorry. I didn't know."

"It's okay. I thought you should know why it's so important to me."

"I'll never make a promise to you or Gabriel I can't keep. In fact, besides you, Gabriel is one of the reasons why I came over. What day can he and his friends fly to Disneyland? I'll take them all tomorrow if he wants."

Courtney looked at Carter through eyes glistening with tears. "You're forgiven. We'll let Gabriel pick the day."

"Courtney, I wish I would have known this about you. I would never have made the promise."

"Since I'm confessing, I need to tell you I have a problem with rejection."

"Most people have that problem. Nobody likes rejection."

"But I've been like this all of my life Carter. It comes from my childhood."

"What happened to cause this?"

"As I told you before when I was growing up, my mother didn't value me for myself. She valued me for my accomplishments, or how I performed in school. My sister refused to perform for my mother, so she rebelled and decided to throw her life away on drugs."

"I'm sorry, Courtney."

"One of the reasons I'm so overprotective of Gabriel is because I'm afraid my sister is going to try to take him back."

"I told you not to worry about that. You sister will have to go through me and the entire judicial system to take Gabriel from you."

"Anyway, all my life I believed my mother would love me if I became successful in my career. That's why I couldn't let her know I had lost my job and my house. If she found out, then she would reject me and give me a disapproving look. I can't stand to see her look at me that way."

"You don't have to tell me all of this."

"Yes, I do, Carter. I want you to know the real me. My problem with rejection spilled over into my adult life. I may initiate a relationship, but then end it before the other person gets to know me well, I end it. That's what I did to you. I tried to end our relationship before you got to know about my issues."

"Issues. Tell me about it. I have my issues too. The reason I withdraw sometimes is because when I was growing up, I felt crowded out by my brothers. I ended up alienating my family and withdrawing into my own world. The reason I've never been in love is because, I alienated women, until I met you. The reason I open up to you, Courtney is because you've shown me a different side of life. I used to make money my God. But I can't image doing that now that I know you. The way you love Gabriel and your students at the school have taught me how to love."

"Yes, but you made me think about the destructive nature of pride."

"You have your problem with pride, and I have my problem with love. Do you think we can ever get past our issues? Because I never realized how much, I loved you until we were separated." Carter confessed.

"I'm willing to try, Carter."

"Promise me you will stop performing for anyone, especially for me. I want to love you for the imperfect, vulnerable, human being you are, and nothing else."

Courtney broke down and started to cry. "No one has ever said anything like that to me before. I'm touched and amazed by your kind, loving ways Carter. I will try and understand your issues, Carter. Your hurts and triumphs are intensely real to me. I never realized how much I loved you either until you were gone. I promise to compromise on our issues," Courtney admitted.

Carter put his finger to her lips. "I'm willing to

work on our issues so long as we are together." Carter swung her into the circle of his arms and planted a tantalizing kiss on her lips. There was a dreamy intimacy to their kiss now that their love had deepened. Neither of them wanted to stop, but Carter heard Gabriel's voice.

"Can I come out now Auntie Courtney? I finished my homework."

"Yes. You can come out."

Gabriel ran out and squeezed between them. He handed Carter his Toy Story book and said, "I like the way you read this book to me, Uncle Carter. Will you read it to me tonight before I go to bed?"

"You better ask your Aunt Courtney."

"Can Uncle Carter read this book to me? Please Auntie Courtney, please."

"Of course he can."

"I love you, Auntie Courtney. And I love you, Uncle Carter."

"I love you too buddy. Now, I have one question for you?"

Gabriel gave him a perplexed look.

"When can you and your friends fly to Disneyland?"

"I'm ready to go now."

"Well you and your Auntie ask your friends, and I'll prepare the flight."

"Thank you, Uncle Carter. Thank you." Gabriel said leaning his head on Carter's shoulder.

Carter began reading Toy Story.

***

Carter helped the driver pack the children's bags into the rented bus while Gabriel and his friends, including Jamal, from the After School Program, sat around the kitchen table swirling pancakes around in syrup. It was the Martin Luther King holiday, and most of the children spent the night at Gabriel's sleepover, the other children, mostly girls, filed in one by one, with their parents who agreed to help with chaperoning. Excitement filled the air as chattering children laughed and talked about what they were going to do at Disneyland.

"I want to get on the submarine ride," Gabriel said to Jamal.

"I want to ride in the tea cups," a little girl said as she entered the house.

"Boy Gabriel, I wish I had a father like Mr. Underwood to take us to Disneyland."

"He's not my real father, but maybe he can be

like a father to you too."

"Jamal looked down at his sneakers. It was nice of him to buy me these shoes and clothes. My real father never bought me any clothes."

"Yeah, he's pretty good. I think I'll keep him. Just think no homework for the whole weekend. Only fun!" Gabriel said.

Courtney busied herself cleaning the kitchen behind the children when she saw two mothers walk in with her daughters. "Thank God you're here. Can you help get the children washed up and get ready to board the bus?"

Both women went to the table and removed empty plates and glasses. After they had cleared the table, one mother made sure each child washed his or her hands in the bathroom while the other mother stood at the door making sure each child had his or her winter coat before filing out the front door.

Minutes later, Carter honked the horn. "Come on people. Let's go."

Courtney started the dishwasher and snatched her handbag before locking the front door. "I'm coming Carter."

Carter sat across from the bus driver on the way to the Oakland Airport where he had his private jet waiting. After a few minutes, Courtney and the mothers stood up and handed each child a small coloring book and crayons to keep them occupied during the ride.

Carter texted Tre, his account manager at Air Charter Service, "Is the jet at the airport and ready for the children to board? We'll be there in about ten minutes."

Tre texted him back, "The jet is gassed up at the airport and waiting for the children."

Once the bus pulled up to the corporate airfield, Gabriel gasped. "Wow. Look at that big jet," Gabriel said to Jamal.

"It looks like a fighter jet out of Star Wars," one boy said.

"I've never seen a plane that big before," Jamal said.

"You've never seen a plane at all," a little girl said turning around in her seat.

Jamal rolled his eyes at the girl.

"All right now. Be nice!" a mother warned, giving the little girl a serious look.

As all of the children exited the bus wearing puff jackets in a rainbow of colors, they stood in line by the plane with the mothers waiting to board.

Once the stairs lowered from the plane and the pilot and steward stood at the door the children yelled, "Yay." They threw up their hands like they were at a football game while the bus driver and his helpers, loaded the plane with luggage.

Carter stood by supervising every move of the bus driver and his helpers to ensure they loaded all of the bags in the plane. After the bus had pulled off, Carter walked down the line of children rubbing heads, slapping them high fives and giving hugs to each one of them. Courtney followed close behind him. Carter said to Gabriel, "Let's get on last, Buddy. I have something to ask you."

After all of the children boarded the plane, Carter asked Gabriel. "Did I do well, Son?"

Gabriel walked into Carter's arms. "You did well, Uncle Carter. Today has been the best day of my life."

With tears in her eyes, Courtney hugged Carter and Gabriel in a tender moment of them all bonding together like a family.

Carter whispered to Courtney and Gabriel, "This is the best day of my life too."

Chapter 16

Six months had passed, and Carter continued to hold the office of Chairman of the Board and attended monthly board meetings. He worked full-time in the winery running the bottling operation. Within six months, he had successfully increased the profits of the winery, by increasing the speed of the bottling process. The winery now produced several varieties of white and red wines. He and Kenton planned to produce champagnes and sparkling wines shortly.

Word got around about Reginald' disloyalty to Underwood Technologies. Now he was working as a cut throat man for a Silicon Valley start-up to bring in more money.

Sandeep continued to run Underwood Technologies. He hired new biomedical engineers to develop new medical devices that would take years of testing to get approval to release on the market. Sandeep also established an intern program, especially for urban youth.

Courtney's After School Program became a model for the entire school district. She enrolled many of her students into Sandeep's Urban Intern Program at Underwood Technologies.

One day when Carter and Courtney were in the

middle of planning their wedding, Carter said, "Thank you for healing my heart condition."

"What heart condition?"

"Before I met you Kenton told me my heart was in scrap condition. You healed my heart and taught me how to love."

Courtney leaned her head on Carter's shoulder. "I love you, Carter."

***

After a year, Carter and Courtney were married in Hawaii in a breathtaking Honolulu Chapel designed with a "diamond" theme and a panoramic view under a glass skylight that radiated and sparkled in the sun, creating a sophisticated view of a beautiful beach.

With their backs toward the ocean, Kenton, Justin, and Brandon stood on the left side of the minister as Carter's groomsmen. Ashley, Melanie, and Crystal stood on the right side of the minister as Courtney's bridesmaids wore violet silk organza gowns.

Carter and Courtney walked hand-in-hand toward the aqua colored ocean. Courtney wore a billowy white organza wedding gown and veil, floating in the warm Hawaiian breeze. She carried a bouquet of violet orchids.

They stood in front of Henrietta's minister taking their wedding vows. Gabriel handed Carter the ring on a little white pillow. After saying their vows, Carter took the ring and placed it on Courtney's left hand, third finger and lifted the veil. He kissed his bride, and took Gabriel by the hand, ready to begin living an everlasting life of love and happiness.

They had their reception and luau on an oceanfront beach at a private estate surrounded by fragrant tropical flowers. All of the guests wore orchid flower leis around their necks and clapped as the couple entered as Mr. and Mrs. Carter Underwood.

The guests sat on the patio at round tables draped in elegant lavender table cloths. Soft Hawaiian music filled the air as servers brought plates filled with Asian and Hawaiian luau cuisine to the guests. Carter, Courtney, and Gabriel sat at the head table along with the rest of the wedding party.

The guests included people Kenton, and Briana had invited from several wineries, restaurants and City officials. Victoria Sutton and her family from Sutton Bed and Breakfast were in attendance. Justin and Ashley had invited a host of civil rights activists, and some of Ashley's customers from her Day Spa. Brandon and some of his artist friends were in attendance, and Crystal and her best friend from UC Davis were in attendance. Everyone ate and drank and watched the Hawaiian sun sink into the blue Pacific Ocean.

Henrietta sat in her wheelchair with her nurse at her side and said, "three down, two to go."

THE END

THE UNDERWOODS OF NAPA VALLEY SERIES

Kenton's Vintage Affair Book 1

Briana Rutledge inherits a cottage on one thousand acres of land in California's Napa Valley Wine Country making her a millionaire. She sets out to turn the cottage into her dream restaurant. Others have agendas to destroy Briana and prevent her from opening her restaurant. Betrayed by his ex, vintner, Kenton Underwood, has been scarred by an obsession that fuels his competitive behavior.

Justin's Body of Work Book 2

Ashley Jacobs relishes in providing her customers with a soothing and healing environment at her day spa in Napa Valley. But when she faces a vicious lawsuit, from someone she least suspects, her peace of mind comes to a complete halt. Justin Underwood is a modern day knight in shining armor, who fights for the disenfranchised in court. After taking Ashley's case, he watches her turn a blind eye to her enemies behind her lawsuit

Carter's Heart Condition Book 3

Billionaire Carter Underwood wants to travel the world to get a new perspective on life. He's used to controlling his time, money and his heart until he meets the former "Miss Oakland," Courtney Oliver, a fourth grade teacher. After meeting Courtney, Carter transforms from a self-centered CEO to a happy, smiling man in love for the first time in his life. But Courtney has a secret that prevents her from believing anyone could ever love her

About The Author

Janice L. Dennie is an Amazon bestselling author of women's fiction and romantic novels. Her books include, The Underwood's of Napa Valley Series and The Lion of Judah Series.

She released her newest novel, Carter's Heart Condition on December 1, 2015 and a novella, Tisha's Warm Christmas, on November 1, 2015. She is currently working on Book 4 of The Underwood's of Napa Valley Series.

The books in The Underwood's of Napa Valley Series have all made Amazon's Top 100 Bestsellers list in AA Literature in the Romance category in 2015.

The Lion of Judah was listed in Amazon's Top 100 Bestsellers list in AA Literature in the Romance category and World Literature in the African category during its initial release in 2015.

Janice was born in Denver, Colorado and raised in Northern California. After graduating from college, Janice began a career with a federal agency. Currently, she writes full-time and lives in Northern California with her family.

Visit her online at http://www.janicedennie.com where you will find a full listing of her novels, upcoming novels and contact information.

www.ingramcontent.com/pod-product-compliance
Lightning Source LLC
Chambersburg PA
CBHW020406150626
46554CB00012B/352